Heartless
Love

Heartless Love

From the Editors
Of *True Story* And
True Confessions

Published by True Renditions, LLC

True Renditions, LLC
105 E. 34th Street, Suite 141
New York, NY 10016

ISBN: 978-1-938877-81-0

Visit us on the web at www.truerenditionsllc.com.

Contents

BETRAYED
I slept with my best friend's man

Chevonne was my best friend, and I loved her dearly. I didn't mean to betray her—it just happened. I know that people say nothing just "happens" but I swear, I would never have hurt her intentionally. My only excuse was that I fell in love. Unfortunately, it was with her man.

This wasn't like me. I didn't go after other women's men. But when T. J. Watkins looked at me with his luscious velvety brown eyes, something stirred deep within my soul. I was a goner. I knew I should have resisted. I knew I should have stayed strong. There was no two ways about it; I should have kept my mitts off her man. But I didn't.

When I saw Chevonne in the hallways at school, she wouldn't talk to me. She wouldn't even look at me. When I tried to call her, she just would hang up the phone. If her mother or brothers answered, they'd say she wasn't there, but I knew she was.

Do you miss me as much as I miss you, Chevonne? I thought to myself. What I was experiencing was an agony that I couldn't begin to express, a pain that wouldn't go away.

I wish that I could turn back the clock and change what happened. But I couldn't. The only thing I could do is hate myself for being such a stupid, lovesick fool. I lost the best friend I ever had because I was blinded by passion.

Was T. J. Watkins, the godlike creature, the object of my desire, worth the sacrifice of a ten-year friendship? I wish that I could say he was, but after playing me for a fool, he moved on. I have nothing to show for my stupidity except a lot of self-loathing and the pain of a broken heart. My heart had been broken twice—once, by my best friend, Chevonne, and once, by the man I had thought I loved. A man who turned out to be a cocky, good-for-nothing loser.

It all started innocently enough. I was watching Chevonne cheerleading at the basketball pep rally when T. J. suddenly appeared beside me. There was nothing underhanded about it—he needed a place to sit. We were just friends. He and I were both there to cheer on the team, or so I'd thought at the time.

Was it just a coincidence that he'd sat down beside me that day? I didn't know, but I couldn't keep my eyes off him.

If I had known then what I was later to learn, I would have picked up myself off the bleachers as fast as I could and headed straight for the door. But, of course, I had no idea what fate had in store for me, when I looked up and saw T. J. Watkins standing there.

"Hey there, Shelby," he said. "Mind if I sit with you?"

"No, come on and sit down," I said, scooting over. He squeezed in beside me, offering me some popcorn. There were a lot of kids at the pep rally. The crowd poured behind us.

"Did I miss much?" he asked, tossing a kernel and catching it in his mouth.

"No, just Mr. Boone's speech," I replied.

"Good!" T. J. grinned. "That was perfect timing."

I grinned back at him. Mr. Boone, our principal, was known for his long-winded speeches.

As far as I was concerned, T. J. and I were just a couple of friends enjoying a pep rally, while we watched Chevonne and the other girls leading the cheers. We were yelling our hearts out, imbued with school spirit. I had no designs on him, no ulterior motive. After all, he was my best friend's man.

I'll admit that my heart skipped a beat when his arm accidentally brushed mine. And, I did notice his cologne. One whiff of that cologne would have set any woman on fire. And yes, I noticed his perfectly aligned white teeth—I had a thing about teeth. And those lips! They were so sumptuous, so perfect for kissing. He had some manly physique! What girl wouldn't go crazy over that?

His voice was so low and sexy that he could have given Barry White a run for his money. And, the way he looked at me set my pulse racing.

I'd never seen him that close before. Oh, I'd seen him with Chevonne all the time, of course, laughing and holding hands, but I'd never really paid that much attention to him He was Chevonne's man. I knew it and the world knew it. Who paid attention to other girls' boyfriends? We had a name for girls like that, girls who tried to steal other girl's guys, and it wasn't a nice one.

Of course, before Chevonne got him, I'd admired him from afar, as all the girls at Columbus High had. It was like the crush you have on a movie star—a nice little fantasy, with no possibility of coming true. I'd known that he was handsome, but being that close to him had sent my emotions into orbit.

He was gorgeous, there was no denying it. Never in a million years would I have gone after him without some encouragement. I was not excusing what I had done. I tried to explain it so that it would have been straight in my own mind.

I hadn't set out to steal him. The whole idea was ludicrous. What would he want me for, anyway? Chevonne was Whitney Houston; I was Queen Latifah. Chevonne was champagne and caviar; I was beer and chips. No man in his right mind would go after me when he could have Chevonne. It wouldn't have made any sense.

So I sat there, pretty as you please that Wednesday, all sunshine and innocence, with no foreboding, no inkling of what was to come.

We were laughing, talking, and having a good time. So what? So what if I liked the way he smelled, the way he leaned in to me real close. I told myself that it didn't mean anything. He was just trying to get a better look at Chevonne.

"Chevonne's looking good out there," I said admiringly, watching her climb onto the top of a pyramid formation consisting of two girls on their knees balancing on the backs of two other girls. If I'd have tried that, the pyramid would have collapsed in two seconds flat, but Chevonne stood aloft effortlessly, hands on her hips, a triumphant smile on her face. The crowd went wild.

"Looking good," T. J. murmured in my ear. I could feel his breath, hot and heavy on my cheek. The hairs on the back of my neck prickled. I should have paid attention to my instincts. The man was coming on to me. I should have put him in his place then and there, but I didn't. Maybe a secret part of me was thrilled. Thrilled that a man like that could want someone like me. So I pretended that I didn't catch his meaning, figuring that if I didn't respond to it, I didn't have to stop it.

The rest of the rally was a haze to me. The coach said a few words—an inspiring speech, I imagine—but I didn't hear a word of it. Then, the members of the basketball team were introduced, with drums and fanfare. Each jock ran out onto the gym floor as his name was called, joining his teammates. Then there were a few more cheers, and it was over.

Chevonne ran over to us, happy, excited. She reminded me of an irritating, chirpy bird. T. J. slipped his arms around her waist like he always did, like he'd done a hundred times before. It had never fazed me a bit. I'd always just seen it as a guy and his girl—a natural show of affection. Only that time, a really weird thing happened, something totally unexpected. I felt jealous.

There was Chevonne, hanging all over her boyfriend, a thing that she had a perfect right to do, and I felt jealous. Of course, I didn't admit my feelings, even to myself. I pretended that I didn't care that she was kissing T. J., but all the while, that green-eyed monster was eating me whole.

I began sitting with T. J. at the basketball games after that. It's perfectly natural, I told myself. We were both sitting in the cheering section, anyway—we might as well sit together.

I had always enjoyed the basketball games. A bunch of sweaty hunks running around in their little shorts was my ideas of a good time. I had another reasons for enjoying the games so much. I lived for the games because they were my chance to see T. J.

3

Of course, it was all subconscious on my part, you understand. I told myself that the reason I was so excited about the games was because we had such a good team that year. In reality, at the end of the game, half the time I wasn't even sure of who'd won.

I started experimenting with the latest shades of eye makeup, and the newest lip glosses. I'd never really bothered with makeup before. There really wasn't any point to it. If you still weren't traditionally attractive after putting on foundation that guaranteed a smooth, even toned, kissably soft complexion, you would be out of luck.

T. J. actually seemed to like me. He seemed to want me. And nobody had ever wanted me before, except Howie Treacher, the nerd of all time, and he didn't count.

I had been on a zillion diets. None of them worked, of course, but it wasn't for lack of trying. I tossed down grapefruit tablets, fat-blocker pills, and appetite suppressants. I drank so much water people thought that I was a water buffalo. I lived on salad greens and soybeans.

I tried jogging, aerobics, jump ropes, tae bo and tai chi. I watched my yoga tape so often that I was in danger of becoming a human pretzel. I racked up miles on the treadmill. At the end of my diet and exercise regime, I'd lost a grand total of two pounds and then, I promptly regained the two pounds I had lost and gained seven more. There was no justice in the world.

I told Chevonne I was on a self-improvement and health kick, and she believed me. She never suspected that it was a crazy, pitiful effort to get her man. I wouldn't even acknowledge it to myself. Oh, maybe somewhere deep down in my psyche, I couldn't admit it to myself, because then I would have to face what a horrible, contemptible creature I really was.

I knew there was no future in my crush on my best friend's boyfriend. He'd never leave Chevonne. And I really didn't want him to do it, either. The most I could ever hope for were a few moments of stolen pleasure when I looked into his baby-brown eyes.

I was living a life of vicarious thrills, consumed with guilt, but I couldn't seem to stop. It was like an addiction. I was beginning to panic, because the basketball season would soon be over, and then what would I do? Like an addict, I had to have my fix. Without it, my life would be pure hell.

And so I suffered, knowing that the end was at hand. Basketball season inexorably drew to a close, and I had to content myself with glimpses of T. J. here and there, always on Chevonne's arm. It was maddening. He was so close and yet, so far away. I thought he winked at me once, when Chevonne wasn't looking.

I never saw him alone anymore. He was always with Chevonne.

4

Of course, that was as it should be, I reminded myself. I knew that I should have just given up on my insane crush, but somehow, I couldn't.

My grades began to slip. I had always been an excellent student, but it was hard to concentrate when all I could do was mope around. Even food had lost its appeal to me. Normally, I would have been thrilled with that unlikely phenomenon, but I found that suddenly, it didn't make a bit of difference to me. What was the use in being thin when you'd lost the one person you wanted to be thin for?

And, that's when it happened—the chance of a lifetime. It was fate, pure and simple. And the craziest thing of all was that my best friend, in her innocence, had set the wheels in motion.

"I've got to go out of town this weekend," Chevonne told me when we were standing at her locker one Friday. "My Aunt Clotilde out in Florida just died. I have to go to her funeral."

"Oh, I'm sorry," I said. "I didn't know you had an aunt in Florida."

"I didn't really know her very well," Chevonne explained. "She came to a few of the family reunions, and once we went to Disney World for a vacation and stopped off at her house for a visit. She used to send me birthday cards when I was a kid."

"When are you leaving?" I asked.

"Tonight," she told me.

"You're going to miss the sports banquet on Saturday," I pointed out. The annual all-star school sports banquet was always a big deal to the students at Columbus. Some of the parents of the jocks had a lot of money, and they always donated generously to the occasion. It was a dress-up affair, with a lot of food. I had gained five pounds at the last one. The lucky girls who had dates took them, while the rest of us went stag.

"Oh, that's right," Chevonne said. "I hate to miss that. I have to go to this funeral, though. She shrugged.

This is going to be a drag, I thought. It wasn't exactly a thrill to tag along with Chevonne and T. J. to the banquet, but at least with them, I'd have had somebody to talk to during the evening. I pictured myself sitting forlornly at one of the long banquet tables, eating alone, surrounded by laughing, happy kids. I certainly wasn't looking forward to that.

"Say, do you have your ticket yet?" Chevonne asked.

"Nope, I was just going to get it at the door," I told her.

"Use mine," she urged. "There's no need for a perfectly good ticket to go to waste."

"Thanks, but I think I might just pass on the banquet this year," I said.

5

"Oh, no, don't do that!" she protested.

"It won't be any fun without you."

"I'll feel bad if you don't go just because I can't," Chevonne said. "It's going to be the social event of the season."

"But I hate to go alone—"

A thought suddenly struck her. It was like a thunderbolt from above. She dug in her purse and withdrew two rumpled tickets.

"Why don't you go with T. J.?" she asked. "I've got his ticket right here. I'm sure that he won't mind."

I stood there, staring at the two tickets she was offering.

"What's the matter?" Chevonne asked. "You like T. J., don't you?"

"Yes," I admitted. "But he's your boyfriend."

"Relax, it's not a date or anything," she told me with a giggle.

"No," I said slowly, swallowing hard. "It's not a date."

"I trust you," Chevonne said. "After all, what are you going to do, go behind my back and try to steal my man?" she joked.

"Never that, girlfriend," I joked back, laughing weakly.

"I'll tell T. J. to pick you up tomorrow night at seven," she said.

"Seven it is," I agreed, stuffing the tickets into my pocket, knowing that my fate was sealed.

I stood in front of my closet that night, clothes strewn everywhere, agonizing over what to wear to the banquet. Usually it took me about ten minutes to pick out something to wear to the banquet—a nice blouse and a nice pair of pants. But this time everything was different. I was trying to find something cute but alluring. The trouble was, I didn't own anything like that. As far as clothes were concerned, I'd always focused more on comfort than on style.

Maybe I could find a pretty dress to wear, I thought. I searched through all of my dresses, which was easy enough to do because there were only a few. I only wore dresses to church. They were all woefully out of date. They were all right for the Lord to see, because He didn't care what you wore to His House, but not what you'd wear to impress a guy. Not that I was trying to impress anybody, I assured myself. I just felt like dressing up a little for a change. There was nothing wrong with that, was there?

I implored Mom to give me some cash to go shopping for a new dress for the sports banquet.

"Why can't you wear one of the dresses you've got?" Mom asked.

"Those old rags?" I cried.

"You wore one of those 'old rags' just last Sunday, with no complaints," she reminded me.

"This is different. It's the sports banquet!" I protested.

"You've gone to the sports banquet before, and never raised this much fuss," Mom said, puzzled. Then her face lit up in a smile. "Who's going to be at this banquet?"

"Nobody special." I shrugged, ignoring her insinuation. "Just the usual kids—pep club members, cheerleaders, jocks."

"Well, I guess you can have a new dress. Let me speak to your father. Since it's for a special occasion, maybe he'll let you use the credit card."

"That would be great. Thanks, Mom," I said, giving her a hug. "Oh, by the way," I added casually, "T. J. Watkins is going to pick me up."

"T. J. Watkins? Isn't that Chevonne's boyfriend?" Mom asked curiously.

"Yes, Mother," I replied. "Don't look at me like that. It's not a date or anything. We're just friends. Chevonne can't go, so she gave me her ticket."

"Of course," Mom said smoothly. "I knew that. What else could it be? You'd never steal your best friend's boyfriend."

"Of course not," I said with a nervous laugh. "I wouldn't do a thing like that. I'm just helping out Chevonne, keeping an eye on T. J. There are a lot of man-hungry females out there, you know."

Mom grinned. "T. J.'s quite a looker, isn't he?"

"Really?" I shrugged. "I hadn't noticed."

After a long, exhausting Saturday morning and afternoon of shopping, I found the perfect dress. It was black satin and very sleek. It was simple but sophisticated, and definitely alluring. I was thankful that the dress manufacturers were finally getting the message and making more attractive clothes in plus sizes. It made me feel like a princess when I tried it on in the dressing room. I stood there, staring at my reflection in the mirror, imagining the look that would be on T. J.'s face when he saw me in it that night. My mind drifted off into a fantasy that I'd never allowed myself to have before. . . .

Suddenly, I imagined what it would be like to have T. J. touch me. I could almost feel the heat of his hands on my aching breasts, and my body started to tingle in anticipation. I imagined those lips of his parting, and his soft, wet tongue tracing a path down my body, which was glistening with desire. I thought of how it would feel to be one with him, how it would feel to have his manhood inside of me, making me whole—making me a woman. I imagined our bodies, slick with desire, doing forbidden things to one another, and not being able to stop the fires that were raging within us. . . .

In my head, I imagined how he would engulf my nipples with his delicious tongue, teasing me as I begged him to deliver his body to me in that special way lovers did. His strong, firm arms would grasp my delicate waist and squeeze me until my body was hot and ready. In the heat of passion, he'd thrust his manhood deep inside me, turning my moanful cries into screams of incredible delight. I shuddered at the thought of our sweet climax, his own cries of joy would be too much for us to handle.

Then, all of a sudden, in the midst of my reverie, I felt ashamed.

What am I doing? I asked my reflection. I should call T. J. right now and cancel. I can't do this to Chevonne. She's my best friend. It isn't right. I should stop this all right now, before it goes any further, before the damage is done.

But instead of heading for the door and the nearest phone, like I should have, I took the dress to the counter and paid for my purchase. Somehow, I knew, in the deepest, secret recesses of my mind, that nothing on earth could have stopped me from going to the banquet with T. J. that night.

After my arduous shopping expedition, instead of the usual quick shower, I took a long, luxurious soak in Mom's rose-scented bath oil. The image of Chevonne's face floated unbidden to my mind, and I pushed it away, determined that nothing would spoil my night.

I was in a tizzy preparing for the banquet. Seven o'clock was rolling around mighty fast and I wanted to look absolutely perfect.

Naturally, I couldn't do a thing with my hair. Sometimes, I believed that it had a mind of its own. Usually it didn't bother me too much, though. I just stuck a few clips in it and hoped for the best.

No matter what I tried, it didn't work, so I finally had to give up. I comforted myself with the knowledge that even though my hair was a disaster, I had definitely made the right decision as far as the dress was concerned.

Cinderella, eat your heart out, I thought as I twirled in front of the full-length mirror.

My makeup looked good, too. I'd splurged on a new tube of lipstick and black mascara for the occasion. When I finished my machinations at the vanity table, I was amazed at the transformation. Plain old Shelby Graham had suddenly become a beauty queen.

Mom looked startled when she saw me. "Who is this voluptuous creature that has taken over the body of my daughter?" she teased, whipping out her camera to take a picture.

"Cut it out, Mom," I said, blushing. Secretly, though, I was pleased.

Then, the doorbell rang.

"Wait," I cried, running out of the room as Mom went to open the door. I wanted to make a grand entrance.

I hid in the hallway while Mom ushered T. J. into the room. He was looking very suave in a black suit. He was even wearing a tie. I'd never seen T. J. in a tie before.

His jaw nearly fell to the floor when he saw me. "You look beautiful," he breathed.

I smiled happily. T. J.'s reaction was worth every second of the stern lecture I knew I'd receive when my dad got a look at the bill for the dress, which had greatly exceeded the spending limit that he had given me.

T. J. handed me a bouquet of six long-stemmed roses wrapped in plastic, tied with a big pink bow. I bent down to smell the wonderful aroma.

"Thank you," I said, handing them to Mom to put in water. I had never gotten roses from a guy before.

I grabbed my little black beaded evening bag, which I'd borrowed from my friend, Rachel, and wrapped my new black scarf around my shoulders. I'd bought it with my baby-sitting money. Then, we were off, my shiny black heels—the ones which were usually reserved for Sundays—clicking smartly on the sidewalk.

Everything would have been perfect, a dream come true, had it not been for the tiny, nagging voice in the back of my head which was accusing me, berating me. I tried my best to ignore it. After all, I wasn't doing anything so terrible, I reasoned with myself. Chevonne had wanted me to go to the banquet with her boyfriend. It had been her idea. In fact, she'd insisted that I go with him, hadn't she?

But deep down, I knew the truth. Try as I might, I couldn't escape the sordid, ugly facts. I wasn't doing anybody any favors—except maybe myself. I wasn't going to the banquet because Chevonne had wanted me to go. I was going because I wanted to go. And I'd never wanted anything so badly in my life.

Like the perfect gentleman, T. J. opened the front door, passenger side, and I climbed into his gleaming car. Well, it actually belonged to Mr. Watkins, T. J.'s father. T. J. got to borrow it for special occasions. I'd seen Chevonne riding in it once or twice. In lieu of a carriage with white horses, it was a suitable vehicle to transport Cinderella to the ball. I looked back at the house as we drove off. Mom was standing at the doorway watching us with a strange look on her face.

Columbus High was all lit up, and in the silvery night air, the imposing structure did indeed look like a castle My heart swelled proudly as T. J. took my arm and led me inside. There were students milling around the corridors, and I noted with satisfaction that many of them stopped and stared at us.

We do make a striking couple, I thought to myself with satisfaction. Maybe I was prejudiced, but I believed that we were the best-looking couple there.

We paused at the doorway to the gymnasium, surveying the scene. I heard an audible gasp run through the crowd.

9

"Isn't that Shelby Graham?" I heard someone say. "What's she doing with T. J. Watkins?"

I knew that I'd have to explain later, of course. I'd have to tell everyone that I was just a substitute. But just for a little while, what harm would it do to pretend otherwise? I figured that they'd know the truth soon enough—why disillusion them so early in the game? Chevonne always got the spotlight. For once in my life, it was shining on me. What could it hurt to let it shine just a little longer? Monday morning, I would return to my usual status, plain old Shelby Graham, shadow of Chevonne LaTrier, but that night, I was Shelby Graham, object of adoration and desire. It was my fifteen minutes of fame, and I intended to enjoy every glorious minute of it.

We took our seats at one of the long banquet tables. I looked around at the decorations that I, a member of the decorations committee, had helped put up just a few short days ago, not having any idea then what that particular banquet would end up meaning to me. On the wall, there were colorful hand-lettered banners, many of them in our school colors, and huge posters of guys and girls engaged in various sports. Streamers hung from the ceiling and balloon bouquets were tied to the chairs. Continuing the color theme, the paper plates and cups were coordinated to match.

People were getting up and going to the buffet table. T. J. and I took our places in line.

"Where's Chevonne?" a girl next to me asked pointedly. I knew that I should have explained then and there that I was pinch-hitting for Chevonne, who had had to attend a funeral, but I didn't.

"Well, she's not here, is she?" I said vaguely. That was true enough, but a more detailed explanation was really in order, if I wanted to stop the school gossips in their tracks. It was obvious that people were getting the wrong idea.

"When the cat's away, the mice will play," someone whispered loudly.

At that point, I definitely should have taken the opportunity to announce, in a loud, clear voice that I was there with T. J. only because Chevonne had asked me to go with him. But somehow, I couldn't bring myself to utter the words. I asked myself later why I didn't at least try to set the record straight. Maybe it would have stopped some of the speculation. But the sad truth was, I was enjoying it too much.

I'd always been big, old, boring Shelby, riding on the coattails of her best friend's fame—the girl who could never get a date. I'd never been the "other woman," the temptress that other women had to hide their men from. I had to admit, the idea was a little intriguing—and flattering.

Normally, the stupendous array of food before me would have

been a great temptation, but that night, I hardly noticed it. I had other things on my mind, not the least of which was the handsome hunk beside me. I automatically picked out a few items, and set them on my plate. I didn't even bother with the desserts, even though they had a wide variety of cookies, cakes, and pies, and even brownies, my all-time favorite.

I sat down beside T. J., picking at my food, tantalizingly aware of how close he was to me. He reached for my hand underneath the table. I sat there in a daze throughout the awards ceremony, inhaling the pungent scent of his cologne into my nostrils, my hand tingling in his. I sat there in the crowded auditorium, not hearing a word of the speeches, oblivious to the applause and the tumultuous cheering all around me. Even though we were surrounded by a boisterous throng, I felt as if we were the only two people in the room.

All too soon, it was over. The last trophy was presented, the last cheer had ended. I knew that I would never forget that night. People were slowly filing out, and T. J. and I strolled along with the rest, his arm tucked firmly against the small of my back. I wished that he would hold my hand again, just as had done under the table, but I knew that it was too much to ask. Anyway, that would really have set the gossips' tongues to wagging, so it was probably just as well.

Still, I thought with glee, it would be something to see the amazement on their faces if we were holding hands!

T. J., the consummate gentleman, opened my car door and made sure that I was settled safely inside before going around to the driver's side. I was sorry that the night was drawing to a close, but, at least, I had my memories. I knew that I would go home and carefully press the half of the ticket that the kid at the counter had handed me back when we'd gone into the banquet into my scrapbook. I'd also put in the program that I'd never even glanced at all night. Of course, a few rose petals from the bouquet that T. J. had give me earlier.

All of a sudden, I realized that T. J. was asking me something. I had been so lost in my reverie that I had not heard a word that he had said. With effort, I pulled myself back to the present.

"Excuse me, T. J., what were you saying?" I asked.

"I was just asking if you had to go home yet," T. J. repeated patiently.

"Well, no," I said, glancing at the clock on his dashboard. "My curfew's not for another hour yet."

"Great," T. J. said, peeling out of the parking lot.

"Where are we going?" I asked.

"Just relax. You'll see," T. J. said mysteriously, and I leaned back in the seat, happy that the night wasn't over yet after all. I wondered idly where we where headed.

Maybe to Mario's, the local teen hangout, I speculated. That would be fun. Or I thought that maybe we were going someplace more romantic, someplace with candlelight and soft music. I closed my eyes, and imagined dancing with T. J., snuggled against his broad shoulder, his arm encircling my waist, floating on air.

Suddenly, the car stopped. I opened my eyes tentatively. All I could see in the sweep of the headlights was a huge expanse of bare ground.

Well, we aren't at Mario's, that's for sure, I thought as I looked around. Neither were we parked in front of a fancy restaurant offering dinner and dancing. In fact, I didn't have a clue where we were. We appeared to be parked on some sort of a precipice, right in the middle of nowhere. T. J. killed the motor and switched off the lights.

"Where are we?" I asked, puzzled.

"Don't you recognize it?" T. J. asked.

"No," I said honestly.

"Let me give you a hint." He waved his arm to indicate an area far below us. "Spectacular view."

I craned my neck and peered down into the dark abyss, staring at the twinkling lights of the city nestled in the cavern below. Then I knew immediately where we were. Muldoon Point, better known as Make-out Point to the local teens. I'd never been there before, but it was legendary.

"Listen, I think we'd better go," I said.

"What's your rush? You said you had another hour yet," he protested.

I didn't like where things were going. I looked around uneasily. I noticed for the first time the shadows of other cars, parked in various secluded spots in the moonlight.

T. J. reached around me and pushed a button that reclined my seat back.

"Do you want a drink?" he offered.

I struggled to sit up. "No, thank you," I declined firmly. "We really should go."

"Come on, Shelby, relax," he urged in a silky tone. "The night is young. How about some sounds?" He slid a CD player out from under the seat, and pretty soon, Luther Vandross was crooning a romantic ballad.

Suddenly, as if floating on a cloud, T.J. slid his pants down and reached his hand over to touch my delicate womanhood. I screamed in delight as he then placed his hand in the top of my dress, caressing my breast delicately. The moonlight cascaded over our soon nude bodies as I allowed T.J. to finally enter me. Over and over again, our rhythmic thrusts rocked the car from side to side. Before long, we had both reached to point of no return.

Just as soon as it began, it was over and T.J. immediately threw his suit back on and peered over at me. There was a nasty grimace on his face, like he had just won a bet. He placed the box of condoms back in his glove compartment.

Could it be that the polite, attentive gentleman I had spent the better part of the evening with was actually a wolf in sheep's clothing?

"You come prepared," I joked nervously.

"I used to be a scout," T. J. murmured, his lips brushing my ear. "What do you say we do it one more time?"

"I've got to get home," I said. "What if somebody sees us here?" We had done enough already.

"Nobody's going to see us. It's dark, and they're all busy," he purred.

"But what about Chevonne?" I asked. Suddenly, my conscience came back.

"What about her? I won't tell if you won't."

Then, he kissed me, only it wasn't like the kiss that I had dreamed of, the passionate, soul-stirring kiss that the hero always gave the heroine in my romance novels. What he was doing was something far more sinister—and far more ugly.

I pushed him off me. "Stop it, T. J.!" I cried angrily. "What do you think you're doing?"

"What's the matter with you?" T. J. demanded, his face flushed. "What are you trying to pull? You're the one who came on to me, remember?"

"What are you talking about?" I asked in astonishment.

"Oh, don't act so innocent with me, Miss High-and-Mighty. You sure can put out the signals, but you just don't want to deliver. Don't act shy now."

"Take me home right now, or I'm walking," I insisted, my voice shaking.

T. J. gunned the motor, gravel flying. "I'll take you home, all right," he said. "Gladly."

I huddled over by the door and hung on for dear life, as far away as I could get from the wild-eyed monster who was driving like a maniac.

"Did you really think that I could want you—a girl as big as a barn?" he jeered. "How stupid can you be? It was all a big joke. They were all laughing at you, laughing at the big fat cow. And I was laughing the loudest of them all."

He dumped me unceremoniously at the curb in front of my house and sped off. I let myself into the dark house, thankful that my parents had already gone to bed. At least I'd been spared the agony of having to pretend that everything was all right.

13

I climbed slowly up the stairs and undressed in the dark, letting my precious new dress slide in a heap on the floor. Even though I had put on my warmest pair of pajamas, the ones with the feet in them, my body felt like ice. I lay there for a long time, shivering in the dark, until the tears began to fall.

I had prayed to God to give me strength to face the ordeal in school on Monday, but it was still the hardest day of my life. I not only had to face all the whispers, innuendoes and ridicule, along with T. J.'s sneering face, but also I was forced to admit to an ashen-faced Chevonne that yes, it was true, I had been with her man up on Make-out Point. I had hoped that by some miracle she wouldn't find out, but sure enough, someone had seen us there. It was Tiana Brady, of course—the biggest gossip in school—who had run to Chevonne with the dirt the minute that Chevonne had set foot in the door of Columbus High on Monday morning. There was no use denying it. As painful as it was, I realized that it was time to come clean.

"Yes, I was there with T. J.," I admitted. "I'm sorry."

"You're sorry?" she asked bitterly. "What are you talking about?"

"But it didn't mean anything. You've got to believe me, Chevonne," I begged. "We were at Make-out Point, yes, but I swear to you, he doesn't want me."

"How can I believe you? How can I believe anything you say?" Her eyes were filled with hurt and fury.

"I've never lied to you," I told her, my voice shaking.

"No, you just conveniently left out a few things, like the fact that you were trying to steal my man. Everybody's talking about it. They're laughing about the way you threw yourself at T. J., the way you flaunted yourself at that banquet. And to think, I gave you the tickets! Like a fool, I gave you the green light, handed him to you on a silver platter. How could I have been so stupid?" she asked.

"You're not stupid, Chevonne," I said miserably, hanging my head. "I am."

"Well, at least we're agreed there," she spat.

"I'm sorry, Chevonne. I—"

"Why did you do this to me?" she demanded. "Did you want him that bad?"

"He was your man, Chevonne. He was always yours," I told her, and I knew that it was true.

"Did you want him that bad?" she repeated, emphasizing each syllable.

I thought of the sleepless nights that I'd spent pining away for T. J., and I remembered all of the longing that I'd had in my heart for him. What a waste! What a terrible, pitiful waste.

"Yes," I said, looking her straight in the eye. "I wanted him that bad."

The gossip died down eventually, but for a while there, I felt like I was wearing the Scarlet A. Everybody spurned me, especially Chevonne. It wasn't as glamorous as I had thought it would be, being the "other woman." In fact, it was downright lonely.

T. J. and Chevonne broke up. They got together again briefly, until she caught him cheating again. I avoided him at school as much as possible, but sometimes, I saw him in the hallways, mocking me.

Looking back, I tried to figure out why I had done it, why I had risked my closest friendship, my reputation, my self-respect. I had been attracted to T. J., yes. But it was more than that. As lame as it sounds, I believed that it all boiled down to the fact that I just wanted to be loved. I wanted to know what it was like to feel a man's arms around me, to feel his lips, gentle on mine. I know that it's no excuse, but it's the only one that I've got.

I've given up trying to call Chevonne. Now, I just sit there and stare at the phone. Someday, I'm hoping that she'll forgive me. Someday, I'm hoping that I'll forgive myself. Until that time, I remain imprisoned in a cell of my own creation, the man stealer of Columbus High. The next time I gave a man a chance I knew I would never repeat the same mistake. As I learned to love myself, I also learned that I deserved my own man, not somebody else's.

THE END

BETWEEN TWO LOVERS
I Wanted My Fiancé And His Best Friend!

Looking up from the long list in front of him, my fiancé, Jake, smiled at me. "Okay, Abby, how does this sound? After we pick your parents up from the airport, we'll take them out to lunch, and then later, dinner. After dinner we could catch a movie or maybe hang out at the student union. Sound good for Friday?"

"Honey, my parents won't be arriving for another three weeks. Don't you think we have a little time before we have to map out a schedule?"

Jake squeezed my hand although he continued to look anxious. "Sorry, honey, I know I must be driving you crazy, but you know I like to plan things in advance. Our graduation is going to be hectic enough. I just want to make sure everything goes perfectly."

I bit my tongue to hold back the large sigh I wanted to let out. Jake was right when he said he had been driving me crazy. Although I was looking forward to graduating from college, and all the activities surrounding it, Jake was taking all of the fun out of it by bugging me with endless details and plans.

"If you just relax, everything will be just fine," I reassured him. "To tell you the truth, I'm more worried about passing finals than I am about graduating itself."

"Speaking of finals, I have a meeting with my study group." Jake glanced at his watch. "And I'm already late. Meet you for dinner later?"

I nodded, feeling more than a little relieved that Jake was leaving. "I'll wait for you in front of the cafeteria."

Tucking his fingers under my chin, Jake leaned across and kissed me full on the lips. With his sexy smile, he winked at me and walked out of the library. Whatever irritation I had been feeling disappeared, and replaced with longing for more of Jake's touch.

I could not believe that I was even dating, much less engaged, to the best looking guy on campus. In addition to his stunning looks, Jake was also one of the smartest people in our class. He was graduating Phi Beta Kappa, and was headed off to Harvard Law School in the fall.

When he proposed on Valentine's Day, Jake told me that he wanted to get married the first week of July. That was so that we would have time for a long honeymoon before we moved to Cambridge in August. At the time, I was simply thrilled at the idea of becoming Mrs.

16

Jake Hoffman. Now, I was having tiny, but nagging doubts that maybe everything was moving too fast.

Looking up at the clock, I realized I was about to be late for my own appointment. I tutored students at the campus writing clinic twice a week. Shoving my books into my backpack, I rushed across campus to the classroom where the clinic was held.

Dashing inside, I sputtered apologies. "I'm so sorry to have kept you all waiting." Looking around, I saw that the room was empty, except for Allen, the other tutor.

Laughing at me, Allen said, "Where's the fire?"

I slumped into a desk and tried to catch my breath. "I thought we would be mobbed since this is nearly the end of the semester and term papers are due."

Allen shook his head. "No one is here yet. My guess is that the rush comes tonight after everyone has had dinner."

I nodded in agreement. "You're probably right. In the meantime, I guess I'll do some studying of my own."

I started to pull out a book to read when Allen said, "You know what Abby? We have been tutoring together all year, but I don't think we've exchanged two words."

I thought for a minute. "You're right again. But then it's usually so busy in here, we don't get much of a chance to talk."

Allen smiled and moved into a desk next to mine. "No time like the present. It would be a shame to have been this close to someone so pretty all this time and not even get a chance to know her."

"Um, well…" Not only did Allen's sudden flirtatiousness disturb me, but so did the nervous way I was reacting. While he was not nearly as handsome as Jake, Allen had soft, sleepy, brown eyes, and full, soft lips. I wondered what they would be like to touch and kiss.

As soon as the thought entered my head, I gasped, not believing I was thinking about kissing someone other than Jake.

"What is it?" Allen looked alarmed.

"Oh, I just remembered I forgot to tell my boyfriend something," I lied.

"You go out with Jake Hoffman, right?"

I nodded in confirmation. "We're engaged. We are getting married in July."

"Married so soon? What's the rush?" Allen wrinkled his nose.

"I don't know," I answered quickly. Allen's blunt question caught me off guard.

"Then don't get married." Allen smiled and folded his arms. "That will give you a chance to see perhaps if you want to marry me."

I laughed, sure that Allen was pulling my leg. "Stop teasing me! Now you said you wanted us to get to know each other, so let's talk seriously."

Allen's face grew solemn. "I am serious, Abby. You don't want to tie yourself down so soon. Our college graduation is only the beginning. Why limit your options by getting married too soon?"

"I've dated Jake ever since we were sophomores. Three years really isn't all that soon."

"But you've only dated Jake," Allen said as he leaned closer to me. "You never gave the rest of us guys on campus a chance."

Allen was so close to me, I could tell he was wearing Polo cologne, the same kind that Jake wore. Except on Allen, it smelled much more tantalizing. The very scent of him drew me closer, as if Allen was something delicious I wanted to taste.

I closed my eyes and tried to regain my composure. When I opened them, Allen was smiling at me, as if he knew the effect he was having on me. I could not believe what was happening to me. I attributed this drama to the late May heat.

"Abby," Allen murmured softly as he put his hands on my shoulders and pulled me to him.

I knew he was going to kiss me, but I was helpless to pull away. I was too attracted to Allen's low, hypnotic voice and full lips. Thankfully, a student walked in just at that moment before we did anything.

"Allen, you said to stop by to get some help...oops, did I come at a bad time?" the student asked.

"No!" I hurriedly jumped out of the desk, away from Allen's embrace. "Allen will help you. I'll be right back."

I ran out of the room and down the hall to the bathroom. Hovering over the sink, I threw lots of cold water on my face. I had no idea what was happening to me. I had not even been the slightest bit attracted to another man since I met Jake. Now here I was, inches away from making out with Allen.

Although I was very confused and wanted to be alone to sort things out, I knew I had to go back and finish tutoring. Fortunately, Allen was busy with the student when I returned, and there was another waiting for me to help her. After that, other students trickled in, so that Allen and I were not left alone for the rest of the two hours we were scheduled to tutor.

As soon as I finished tutoring the last student, I grabbed my backpack and dashed out the door. I wanted to make sure Allen did not have a chance to catch up to me. The last think I needed was to be alone with him again, where I might not have been lucky enough to have someone interrupt.

I started to calm down as I got closer to the cafeteria. By the time I got to its entrance, I had regained my composure completely, which was a good thing because Jake was already there waiting for me.

18

Pointing to the bulletin board, Jake frowned. "They are serving meatloaf. Why don't we grab something from off campus?"

I readily agreed. "The mystery meat in the meatloaf is definitely something I won't miss about this place."

"Walk with me back to my room so I can change." Jake was wearing the same T-shirt and shorts he had on earlier.

We held hands as we walked to his dorm room. Once we got there, I entered his room and locked the door behind me, instead of waiting in the hall like I usually did when he changed clothes.

"Abby?" Jake seemed momentarily startled. However, confusion was replaced with desire once I threw myself into his arms and kissed him full on the lips. My hands glided down his muscular chest and settled on his tight rear.

"What's gotten into you?" he gasped in between kisses.

"I want to make love to my fiancé. Is that so bad?" I asked as I slid my hands underneath his thin cotton T-shirt and lifted it over his head. I immediately started kissing his bare, sweaty chest.

"No," Jake moaned. "Nothing bad about that at all." Still kissing me, Jake unbuttoned my blouse and cupped my breasts in his hands. Gently rolling my nipples around in his fingers, he edged me to his bed and we both sank down on it.

Allen was a distant memory as Jake's mouth moved from nibbling my ear to laying delicious kisses on my throat. Spreading my thighs apart, he settled in between my legs as his lips continued to move down my body. The only time Jake paused in his kisses was when he reached my breasts. My nipples, already hardened by his earlier fondling, became even more erect as Jake kissed them. That caused me to moan and writhe in passion, to which Jake responded by pressing his erection against my thigh even more firmly.

I wrapped my legs around Jake's waist, which brought the tip of his erection nearly close enough to where it would do the most good. "Now," I moaned.

"Not yet, baby. Don't rush a good thing." Jake whispered in my ear, as his hands squeezed my rear end. Kissing me deeply again, Jake continued to grind his erection against me, driving me crazy with desire.

"You drive me nuts, you know that, don't you? I want you so badly," Jake mumbled as he finally entered me.

I screamed as I felt my release almost the instant he entered me. Undetected, Jake moved rhythmically until he experienced a release of his own. By that point, I was filled with so much passion again that Jake continued to rock until I felt a second release.

With a long moan, Jake rolled off of me and onto his back. I turned on my side to face him with a big smile. It was definitely the best sex we had ever had. Jake's dazed, but satisfied expression told me that he agreed.

Still panting, Jake asked, "What brought this on? Don't get me wrong, I love it when you initiate sex. I'm just wondering what I can do to ensure it happens more often."

Not wanting to ruin the moment by talking about what had happened with Allen, I simply said, "I felt like practicing for our honeymoon."

Jake groaned and sat up. "That reminds me. I need to call Dad to make sure he's booked us first class tickets to Hawaii. You have to get them early because July is the middle of the tourist season."

"We're going to Hawaii on our honeymoon?" I asked blankly.

Jake smiled proudly. "I was going to surprise you with the tickets in a couple of weeks, but I guess there's no harm in your knowing now."

I sat up, holding Jake's T-shirt against my naked breasts. "But you didn't ask me where I wanted to go on our honeymoon. Shouldn't I have a say?"

"Don't you want to go to Hawaii?" Jake looked confused.

"Frankly, no, I don't. I was hoping we'd go on a tour of Europe. I didn't go on the class trip to Paris last summer because you wanted me to stay here with you. The least you can do is take me there now."

Jake shook his head. "Abby, I didn't know you wanted to go to Paris that badly. I thought you chose to stay here with me because that's what you wanted."

Grabbing my clothes, I started getting dressed. "Look, it doesn't matter now what happened last summer. However, I do want to go to Paris for our honeymoon, not Hawaii."

Jake's eyes widened as if I had suddenly started talking Greek. "I don't think I'll be able to change our plans. I already put a deposit down on the Hawaii honeymoon package. For all I know, Dad might have already gotten the plane tickets. You see, Abby, it's already planned."

"And you made these plans without telling me?" I shook my head in disgust.

"Most women would be thrilled to be going to Hawaii on a honeymoon," Jake replied in a cold voice. "I didn't think I needed to get your permission to plan a luxury vacation for us."

"You got half of that right. You didn't think!" I snapped. Before he could say another word, I dressed quickly and ran out of his room, suddenly feeling suffocated.

As I left Jake's dorm, it occurred to me that I still hadn't eaten dinner. Although I no longer had an appetite, I wanted to get something to take back to my dorm with me for later. I was standing in line waiting to pay for a sandwich and chips, when someone said "Hello" directly in my ear. Jumping straight into the air, I turned to see Allen grinning at me.

"You scared me!" I yelled.

Allen laughed. "Sorry, about that. Here, let me make it up to you by paying for your snack." He gave the cashier the money before I could protest.

"Thank you," I said awkwardly. "I have to get going."

I was about to walk off in the opposite direction when Allen gently held my elbow. "Abby, please talk to me. We need to discuss what happened this afternoon at the tutoring center."

I reluctantly followed Allen to one of the cafeteria tables. "That was a mistake, Allen. There's nothing more to say."

Allen shook his head stubbornly. "There was something about to happen between us. I just wish you'd give us a chance to pursue it."

"I am engaged to Jake, and have no interest in pursuing anything with anyone else," I said firmly.

Allen raised a skeptical eyebrow. "You sure? You didn't look so happy when you first came in here. In fact, it looks like you had just left an argument. Was it with Jake?"

I nodded, surprised at his perception. "Jake and I had a misunderstanding, that's all. I'm certainly not going to start dating someone else because of it."

Allen smiled slyly. "Not even if your attraction to another man was the cause of the fight?"

I could feel myself stiffen in my chair. "And what makes you think we were fighting about another man?"

I could tell Allen knew that he was upsetting me because his expression turned sympathetic instead of teasing. "Just a guess. Am I right?"

"It's private," I told him.

Eyeing my sandwich and chips, Allen said, "Look, I didn't mean to upset you. Why don't I make it up to you by taking you out for a real meal?"

I was about to turn Allen down, when I saw his eyes narrow and his lips narrow. "What's wrong?"

With his index finger, Allen discreetly pointed behind me. When I turned around, I saw an angry Jake headed our way. He had changed into a sweater and khakis, and looked gorgeous except for the scowl on his face.

Approaching our table, Jake turned his back to Allen and did not acknowledge his presence. "Come on, Abby, let's go to dinner," he said to me in a curt tone.

Although I did not appreciate Jake's rudeness, I tried to stay calm so that a fight did not erupt. "I'm talking to Allen right now. I'll call you later on tonight."

Still ignoring Allen, Jake said, "You and Allen can talk tomorrow. You and I need to get some things straight right now."

I could not believe Jake was being so bossy. He had never disrespected me that way before, either in private or in front of someone. I felt like I was going to die from embarrassment.

Allen started to speak in a low, but dangerous voice. "It seems to me like Abby said she would talk to you later. Why don't you just leave her alone now?"

Finally Jake looked at Allen, and gave him the same expression of disbelief that he had showed me earlier. "I think my fiancé can speak for herself. Is this what you want Abby? For me to leave you alone?"

I nodded miserably, wanting more for the scene to be over than to be left alone with Allen. However, before I had a chance to explain, Jake simply said, "Fine."

Jake turned around and stalked away without a backward glance. With a huge sigh, I slumped in my chair. "What just happened here?"

"Your fiancé saw us and jumped to conclusions," Allen said. "Is that the kind of man you want to marry?"

I was so confused, I wasn't sure what I wanted. Pushing away from the table, I got up to leave, mumbling a good-bye to Allen. He stood up too, as if he was going to follow me, but I held up my hand and gestured for him to stay. Thankfully, Allen respected my wishes and didn't try to follow me.

Leaving the cafeteria, I ended up just wandering around aimlessly as I tried to sort things out. Jake was a natural leader, and as such, was used to giving orders. It wasn't until we got engaged that Jake's take-charge attitude bothered me. In fact, I liked the way he was able to make quick decisions, because it took the pressure off me. I was comforted by the fact that someone else was minding the details while looking out for my best interests.

But it seemed since the engagement, Jake had gotten carried away. With little input from me, he had already planned what we would do during our graduation weekend. His mother was planning our wedding. Now Jake had even chosen where we would go on our honeymoon.

When I returned to my dorm room, I was happy to see there were two messages on my answering machine. I was sure Jake had called to apologize. However, I was disappointed to find that none of them were from Jake, only one from my mother and another from Allen. I was too exhausted to return either call, and went to bed, emotionally spent.

The phone ringing woke me up the next morning, and I anxiously answered it. "Jake?" I asked, sure that he was calling me.

"Sorry," Allen's deep voice rang out over the other end. "It's only me. Were you expecting Jake?"

"Yes," I admitted. "We hadn't talked to each other since dinner last night, and we've never gone this long without speaking."

I heard Allen sigh. "I feel sort of guilty, like I might have played a part in the fight the two of you had. Will you have dinner with me tonight?"

I was about to say no, but Allen continued talking. "I figure you could use someone to talk to right now, and I want to be your friend."

Allen sounded so sweet and sincere, I accepted. "Okay, I could use a shoulder to cry on right about now."

We agreed to meet at my dorm later on that night. I was about to go take a shower when the phone rang again. This time it was Jake, and he sounded just as irritable and cranky as he had the night before.

"I was waiting for you to call me last night. I was surprised when you didn't."

"You were the one being a jerk. Why should I have called you?" I demanded.

"Because you owe me an apology for picking a fight, causing a scene in the cafeteria, and trying to make me jealous by sitting with Allen," Jake replied coolly.

"What about the apology you owe me for trying to run my life?"

"I'm not trying to run your life and you know it. But if that's the way you really feel, maybe I'm not the man for you. Maybe we ought to rethink getting married."

Jake's words shocked me, but I was determined not to show him I was wounded. "Maybe we should," I told him in a neutral voice. "In fact, I have a date with Allen tonight. Maybe he's the man for me." I hung up the phone before Jake could get another word in edgewise.

For the rest of the day, I avoided the places where Jake hung out like the library or the student union. But just because I did not see him did not mean I wasn't thinking about him. I wondered if Jake was really serious about calling off our engagement. Knowing him, he probably was, because Jake was not given to bluffing or saying things he didn't mean. I wasn't sure whether to be relieved that I had gotten rid of a control freak, or to be devastated at losing the only man I had ever loved.

I really didn't feel like going out to dinner with Allen, but I decided to keep my promise. Allen appeared happy to see me when he picked me up. "Hi Abby. Tonight I promise you I'm going to help you forget about all your problems. Want to start by getting a pizza?"

"Why don't we just walk around?" I suggested. "I'm not really hungry."

We started walking towards the baseball diamond, which was a deserted part of campus. I wanted privacy because I didn't feel like seeing anyone, and I didn't want to explain why I was out with Allen and not Jake. As we walked, Allen tried to put his arm around my shoulders, but I shied away from his touch.

We were walking along quietly until Allen pointed to a bench and said, "Why don't we stop here for a second and talk?"

I sat on the bench beside Allen and again he tried to put his arm around my shoulders. This time I didn't pull away. His arm felt warm and comforting. Slowly, my attraction was building.

"Lean back and relax," Allen said softly. "You're so tense."

"If you had been through what I've gone through the last twenty-four hours you'd be tense too."

"Yeah, I know, but it might be for the best, you never know."

"What does that mean?" I asked. "I don't know how Jake's and my separation is for the best."

Allen took a deep breath. "I've wanted to tell you this for a long time Abby, but I've liked you ever since we started tutoring together. I could see you were in love with Jake, and I tried to respect that."

Allen used his arm to draw me closer. "But now that you and Jake are having problems, I think it's time you knew how I really felt. I love you, Abby, I really mean that."

"But you can't…" My protests were muted as Allen's grip on me tightened and he pulled me in for a kiss.

I tried to pull away at first, but the gentle, insistent pressure from Allen's lips was too much to resist. My mouth relaxed, and instead of fighting Allen, I eagerly kissed him back, anxious to feel his lips on mine.

Tangling his hands in my hair, Allen started reigning kisses on my forehead, eyes and cheeks. Returning to my lips again, Allen's kisses were deep and erotic. His tongue swept my mouth in a dizzying, passionate haze. Before I could respond in kind, Allen pulled my head back so that my throat was exposed. Gently biting my neck, Allen kissed me so long and deep, it was as if I was water and he was dying of thirst.

Running my hands through Allen's soft, curly hair, I urged him to continue. His kisses were wild and strong, bordering on violent. I could tell that the passion was rising furiously. But that was not enough for me to tell Allen to stop. He as giving me so much pleasure with his mouth, lips, and tongue, I could feel my eyes rolling to the back of my head.

I was in such a dizzy, sexual haze, I was barely aware of Allen edging me down on the bench so that I was flat on my back and he was on top of me. His hands started wandering from my head and neck

24

down to my chest. At first he cupped and fondled my breasts, then his skillful fingers ran smoothly along my thick nipples.

"Allen, no," I murmured as I tried to maneuver myself out from under him.

Allen used his weight to prevent me from moving. "Come on, Abby, we've come too far to stop now."

"Get off of me!" I said in a stronger tone. "I don't want this anymore."

Allen leaped to his feet so fast, I nearly fell off the bench. "Oh, I get it, you're a tease. You lead me on and then make me stop. I don't have time for games, Abby."

Allen's bitterness took me by surprise. "I'm not playing games," I protested. "I didn't come out here for this. I thought we were going to talk."

"You're about as stupid as the other girls on this campus." Allen shot me a disgusted look. "Why would I bring you all the way out here to talk?"

I stood unsteadily on my feet. "You're the one who's stupid. I thought you were trying to be my friend. Now I know I was wrong to trust you. All this time you've been trying to get into my pants."

"If you weren't so uptight, I'd be in your pants and we'd both be enjoying ourselves right now!" Allen spat back.

Looking at Allen's angry, twisted face, I knew he had been lying about his feeling for me all along. I could not believe I fell for this act, and almost ended up making love to him. Not wanting to antagonize Allen any further, I simply backed away from him slowly.

"Where do you think you're going? Get back here!" Allen made a grab for me, and that's when I took off into a full sprint. I could still hear him cursing and yelling at me even when I had left the baseball diamond.

Trudging back to my dorm, I reflected on the mess I had made of things. Because I had been confused by my attraction to Allen, I had probably blown things with Jake for good. I realized now that my anxiety over our upcoming graduation and wedding probably led me to blow things out of proportion. Any woman in her right mind would love to go to Hawaii. I had no business starting a silly fight with Jake over something like that. I had no idea of how I was going to make things right between us.

When I reached the steps that led to the lobby of my dorm, I was surprised to find Jake waiting for me. Looking genuinely remorseful, he handed me a dozen red roses and simply said, "I'm sorry."

His gesture brought tears to my eyes. It was the first time in our relationship that Jake had ever apologized to me. Usually when we quarreled, I was the first to make amends.

"I've been a complete fool. I wouldn't blame you if you never spoke to me again. But Abby I'm asking, no, make that begging you for another chance."

I took Jake's hand in mine and squeezed. "We both deserve a second chance. I acted stupid too, you know."

"I was coming to talk to you earlier, but I saw you walking off with Allen. That's when I knew you were serious about us splitting up. I couldn't handle the thought of you with anyone else besides me."

"Allen is no threat," I assured him. "I thought he would help me talk through my problems, but instead he turned out to be a jerk."

Jake seemed to catch on to my meaning. "Did he touch you? I swear I'll kill him if he did."

I placed a hand on Jake's arm. "Don't worry about it. We are back together, and we are going to work things out. Trifling people like Allen don't matter."

Jake looked relieved as he wrapped his arms around my waist. "I'm so glad you want us to stay together. I can't tell you how scared I was you were going to tell me that it was really over."

I started to reassure Jake that nothing between us was over, but then he kissed me and I forgot what I was going to say. Feeling Jake's lips pressed against mine made me wonder how I could have been tempted by another man. In Jake's arms was the only place I ever wanted to be again.

While the next few weeks were hectic ones, Jake and I managed to find time to talk seriously about our future. We agreed that he would not be so bossy, but that I also had to be more assertive and ask for what I wanted. The talks calmed my anxieties and I once again began to look forward to a July wedding instead of dreading it.

Jake and I did end up going to Hawaii on our honeymoon. Because he felt bad about making the plans without consulting me, Jake assured me that on our first vacation, we would go to Paris. Actually the destination didn't matter to me. As long as I was with Jake, and we compromised and didn't take each other for granted, I was incredibly happy and satisfied!

THE END

I SLEPT WITH ANOTHER MAN FOR REVENGE!

"**I** can't believe it!" I practically exploded, to no one in particular. "I just can't believe it! He's up to his old tricks! He promised me that he'd never fool around again! How could he do this to me after all we've been through?"

"Whoa, Mary, slow down," Janet said, coming over to my desk with a worried look on her face. "What's going on? Are you talking about Dennis?"

I slammed my purse into the middle drawer of my desk. "Yes, I'm talking about Dennis!" I snapped. "I forgot my car keys this morning, and I walked back into the apartment. He was on the phone making plans for this weekend! He was so busy talking, he didn't even hear me come in or leave again!"

Janet frowned. "Maybe you misunderstood," she replied slowly. "He could have been talking to his mother, or his brother or..."

"Or the President of the United States," I finished for her sarcastically.

She laughed. "Well, it could have been perfectly innocent," she replied. "Now, I know Dennis has cheated on you in the past, but that doesn't make him automatically guilty this time. Remember, that's why you agreed to marry him in the first place – because he swore it would never happen again. He's not going to risk his marriage on an affair that means nothing!"

"I know what he promised me," I said, close to tears. "And I was stupid enough to believe him. He knew how hurt I was when he fooled around with Linda. When he asked me to marry him, he swore he'd be faithful. I trusted him to keep that promise."

"Well, just call him and ask him what's going on," Janet said. "There could be a very simple explanation for this."

"Oh, there is," I said darkly. "But Dennis will never tell me the truth about what's going on. If I confront him, he'll just tell me the same old lies he used to. You know, if I hadn't caught him, red-handed, in Linda's apartment, he'd still be telling me he was 'out with the guys.'"

Just then, the phone on Janet's desk rang. "Look, I have to get to work," she said gently. "But don't do anything stupid. Dennis is your husband now. Give him a chance to explain what's going on before you leap to any conclusions."

Janet answered the phone and I leaned back in my chair. I didn't know if it was a good or bad thing that I was at work. On the one hand, I didn't know if I could concentrate on answering questions all day about insurance. On the other hand, the last thing I wanted to do was think about Dennis and whoever he was fooling around with now.

I closed my eyes and willed myself not to cry. Dennis and I had been married for two years now, and I had thought ours was a good marriage. I loved him with all my heart, and I thought he loved me.

I had known Dennis for more than five years, ever since we'd met at a party. At first, I didn't even like him. He was tall and gorgeous, but he seemed awfully conceited. He came over to me and offered me a beer.

"You're the prettiest woman here," he said bluntly. "I'd like to get to know you better."

I didn't take the beer. "That's nice," I said coolly. "And what makes you think I want to get to know you?"

He grinned at me. "You do," he said confidently. "You just don't know it yet."

I walked away, but I wasn't surprised when he followed me. All night, whenever I turned around, there was Dennis. Finally, I glared at him. "Stop it," I said. "Stop following me! I want you to leave me alone."

"Then go out with me tomorrow night," he said, brushing a strand of hair away from my face.

I stared at him in amazement. "Are you nuts?" I asked. "I just said I didn't want to go out with you."

"How do you know that?" he asked seriously. "Why don't you get to know me first?"

"Look, I only met you ten minutes ago," I replied. "But I can tell you're arrogant and conceited and used to getting your own way. I don't like that in a man and I don't need it."

He smiled. "So, what do you need?" he asked, staring into my eyes.

I shook my head. "I'm not playing that game," I said, a bit angrily. "I don't want to flirt with you like some adolescent girl. We're not in high school."

"No, we're not," he agreed. "And I know when I like someone – when I've met someone special. I think you and I should be together. I want to know what it would take to make that happen."

"You can't make it happen," I answered, turning away. "I don't feel any attraction to you." That part was a lie, but I didn't care. Men like Dennis were simply used to getting their own way, and then moving on.

Dennis grabbed me lightly by the elbow, and made me face him.

"I could make you want me," he said gently. Then, he gave me a soft kiss on the lips. I felt a sudden jolt of electricity course through my body. I shivered slightly and stepped back.

"See?" he whispered softly. "I told you."

"I don't see anything," I said stiffly. "Or feel anything. It was just a kiss."

"Right," he said, raising an eyebrow. "That reaction was just my imagination."

"I'm leaving now," I said, trying to be calm. "It was nice talking to you."

Dennis didn't follow me, and I was both surprised and disappointed when he didn't. All the way home, I felt like kicking myself. I felt like I'd made a fool of myself, even though I didn't know what I could have done differently. Dennis was obviously used to having women fall all over him, and that irritated me.

The next morning, I woke up to the sound of the phone ringing. "Hello?" I answered sleepily.

Dennis' deep voice came over the line. "Good morning, Mary," he said huskily. "I'm right down the street from your apartment at the restaurant. Get dressed and come meet me for breakfast."

I sat up in bed. "What?" I asked in disbelief. "You're where?"

"Don't play hard to get," he said, teasing lightly. "I know you don't have a date for breakfast already."

"I don't," I admitted. "But..."

"You can have anything you want." he interrupted quickly. "Pancakes, sausages, even french toast. I'll pay."

"Gee, what an offer," I laughed, feeling excited in spite of myself. "How can I refuse that?"

"I want to see you," he said, his tone becoming serious. "Please have breakfast with me."

"Okay," I agreed finally. "I'll be there. Just give me a few minutes to get ready."

It was crazy to be so excited about meeting someone for breakfast, but I was. I put on my favorite jeans and my new red sweater. Ten minutes later, I was sitting down across the table from Dennis. I had to admit that he had a good reason to be arrogant and conceited. He was a really good-looking man!

"Thanks for coming," he said sincerely. "I wasn't sure you would. I have a suggestion: let's start all over again. I like you and I think we could have something special together. I'll try not to act like a jerk, and you have to promise to give me a second chance."

I smiled. "Okay," I agreed softly.

Over pancakes with strawberries and whipped cream, Dennis and I started to get to know each other. We lingered over our coffee until the waitress started giving us dirty looks.

"I think we better go," I whispered. "She wants us to leave."

He reached for my hand. "Spend the day with me," Dennis said. "We'll do whatever you want: go to the zoo, or the opera, or the movies."

I had to laugh. "That's a wide range of activities to pick from," I replied. "Where do I start?"

Dennis squeezed my hand lightly. "Mary, you know we have something special going on here," he said quietly. "You feel it, and I know I do. Why waste time? Let's see where it's going."

It seemed stupid to protest, so I simply nodded my agreement. Dennis and I spent the whole day together – walking and talking. We ate lunch in the park, then bought the fixings for a steak dinner, which we cooked at my apartment.

"I've never done this before," I said, as we sat at my dinner table.

He looked puzzled. "Never had a steak dinner?" he asked.

I laughed. "Never spent the whole day with a guy, just doing nothing," I answered. "I mean, this has been really nice."

"It could get nicer," he said softly. "I could spend the night."

I shook my head. "It might be nice," I answered truthfully. "But it would be much too soon."

"Not for me," he replied. "But I understand your feelings. I can be patient."

Dennis kissed me goodnight at my front door. It was soft and slow, and made me tingle all the way down to my toes. It took all the willpower I possessed not to change my mind and invite him to spend the night with me.

For the next few weeks, Dennis and I saw each other constantly. I was falling in love with him a little more each day, and I was pretty sure he felt the same way. It was getting harder and harder to push him away when he started kissing me.

One night, I didn't push him away. Instead, I took his hand and led him into the bedroom. "I think you should stay tonight," I said quietly. "What do you think?"

He grinned. "I think it's about time," he replied. "I love you, Mary."

"I love you, too," I said simply.

Dennis was patient and slow with me. He removed my clothes one piece at a time, touching and caressing each portion of my bare skin when it was exposed. Every touch of his hands and lips felt like pure heaven.

Then it was my turn to undress him. I was nervous, and my hands fumbled removing his clothes. When I had stripped him of everything, I stood back for a minute. "Wow!" I said in awe.

He laughed out loud. "I take it you approve of my body," he said. "I'm glad."

"Maybe that's why I thought you were so arrogant when I met you," I replied honestly. "I suppose a lot of women have told you that you're, well, um, nicely equipped."

"No one's put it quite like that," he answered, amused. "Tell me again how much you admire my equipment."

I didn't have a chance to say anything. Dennis grabbed me and kissed me, hard. I felt my whole body respond to that kiss. Together, we melted onto the bed. Dennis ran his hands possessively over my body. "God, you're gorgeous!" he breathed.

I couldn't talk, or even think, while Dennis was touching me. His mouth traced a path from my neck, to my waiting nipples. I gasped with pleasure as he tenderly sucked and gently bit each one.

His hands cupped my buttocks, squeezing them, until his fingers moved between my legs. I moaned softly, and arched my back instinctively against his touch. All too soon, I felt the ripples of pleasure as I climaxed.

Dennis paused to kiss me, then quickly positioned himself on top of my waiting body. With one powerful thrust, he was inside of me. I gave a small cry of pleasure as he brought himself to a climax. We were both panting and sweating when it was finished.

"That was good," he managed at last.

"Very good," I agreed.

Dennis kissed me. "I love you, Mary," he said softly. "More than I ever thought possible."

I was thrilled. I knew I had found the man of my dreams and he loved me too! I reached up to kiss him, and we ended up making love again. When we finally fell asleep, we were both exhausted and happy.

The next morning, Dennis ran out and got doughnuts and coffee. He came back and handed me a cup of hot coffee and a chocolate-covered doughnut. "This is nice," I said. "I'd like to wake up this way every day."

"Let's move in together," he suggested quickly. "I mean it. Look, we're good together. I can give notice on my apartment today. Think of the money we'll save on rent."

Deep down, I wished that Dennis had asked me to marry him, but I was also thrilled at the idea that he wanted to be with me. "Okay," I said quietly. "I think that's a good idea."

Dennis looked serious. "I'm sorry, Mary," he apologized. "I didn't mean to make it sound like a business deal. I love you. I want to be with you."

Maybe it was too soon to move in together, but I had thought we were happy. I loved coming home to Dennis, and I loved waking up

31

next to him the next morning. We shared the cooking and cleaning, and our interests and tastes were very similar.

We had our fair share of fights, but we usually settled them quickly – in bed! Of course, that was the best part. I never tired of making love to Dennis. He could always please me, physically and emotionally.

But, about a year after we'd moved in together, Dennis seemed to change. He started working longer hours, and he was cool and distant when he was home. It was nothing I could put my finger on, and he denied anything was wrong. All the classic warning signs of an affair were right there, but I ignored them.

That is, until a friend tipped me off that she'd seen Dennis having lunch with Linda Montgomery at a restaurant in town. I was hurt and confused, because Dennis had just told me that he'd been so busy at the office for the last few weeks, he'd been eating lunch at his desk.

I didn't confront him at first, but I became more and more suspicious as time went on. I would call Dennis at work, and he wouldn't be there. He would go out to business dinners, but always be starving when he got home. And there were countless nights spent with "the boys." Oh, there were lots of clues, but I didn't want to believe that Dennis was being unfaithful to me.

Finally, however, I had to know. I waited for one of the nights when he said he was going out for a beer with his friends. It was actually almost too easy to catch them together. I saw Dennis and Linda go into her apartment, and then I waited about 10 minutes before I knocked on the door.

If it hadn't been so horribly painful for me, I would have laughed out loud at the shocked expression on Linda's face when she answered the door. She was dressed only in a bathrobe, and Dennis was standing right behind her in just his underwear. It was obvious I was the last person in the world they expected to see!

"Sorry, I didn't bring a pizza," I said icily. "Maybe I could come in and make a sandwich for the two of you."

Dennis took a deep breath. "Mary, I know what you're thinking," he began. "But there's an explanation…"

"Could it be that you're screwing her brains out?" I asked scathingly. "Or is there really something I'm missing here?"

"I love you," he answered weakly.

I laughed bitterly. "Well, that's wonderful," I said sarcastically. "Some people say it with flowers. You've discovered a whole new way."

I was making all sorts of stupid comments, but my heart was breaking. I had loved and trusted this man, and he had made a fool of me!

I raced home, and threw all Dennis' clothes and belongings into the hall. I was so mad and hurt, I didn't care what the neighbors thought, or even if someone stole them before he got there. In fact, I hoped they would!

Naturally, Dennis tried knocking on the door, and he called me at least a dozen times that night. I couldn't talk to him. I was too hurt by what he'd done. I simply wanted him out of my life.

But, of course, he knew where I worked, and he showed up at me desk the next morning, with a bouquet of flowers in his hand. "You have to listen to me," he said firmly.

I shook my head. "No, I don't," I replied calmly. "I never have to listen to you again. You lied to me, and you cheated on me. I can never trust you again."

"That's not true," he protested. "I know I made a mistake – a big one. I'm sorry. I don't even know why it happened."

"I don't care why it happened," I said. "All this time, you lied to me! You told me you were working late and eating lunch at your desk! I believed you. That's what hurts so much."

"I know," he said. "I'm sorry."

"It's not good enough," I replied truthfully.

Dennis left, but he didn't give up. He sent flowers, candy and jewelry. Every day, I got a card or e-mail from him, saying he was sorry and that he loved me. At first, I ignored all of it. But, gradually, I began to soften.

I was still hurt, but I also loved Dennis. I missed him desperately and I wanted to believe he could change.

Finally, he showed up at my door one night, with Chinese food in one hand, and a box of chocolate-covered cherries in the other. I was about to shut the door, when I suddenly changed my mind.

"Come in," I said, with a small sigh. "Just for dinner. And this doesn't mean I forgive you."

Dennis grinned. "Fair enough," he replied. "I brought your favorite – lemon chicken and fried rice."

"Dennis, bringing me my favorite Chinese food is not going to make up for having sex with another woman," I said, a bit impatiently. "The fact is, you lied to me. I don't know if I can get past that, no matter what you say now."

Dennis grabbed both my hands in his. "Listen to me, Mary," he said urgently. "I made a big mistake. I know that now. I knew it then. I don't know what I was thinking about, except maybe I was scared of how much I loved you."

"You loved me so much, you slept with someone else?" I asked in disbelief. "Is that what you're saying?"

"No, no," he answered. "I was afraid of being too dependent

on you. I guess I was trying to figure out if you were as perfect as I thought you were."

"Okay, let's say that for one, crazy minute I bought that story," I said slowly. "What's changed? How do I know you won't do it again? How do you know you won't?"

"Because I love you," he replied simply. "Only you. And I want to marry you."

A few weeks ago, I would have been thrilled at a marriage proposal from Dennis. Now, I could only stare at him in amazement. "I don't know what to say," I answered honestly.

"Don't say no," Dennis said. "Take some time to think about it. I know I did a terrible thing, but it doesn't have to be the end of us. I love you, and I think you still love me."

"I do," I agreed. "But I don't want to be hurt like that again."

"I won't hurt you," he promised. "I'll never cheat on you again. I swear it, Mary."

It took me a week to finally decide I wanted to marry Dennis. I had a lot of doubts, but I also knew I loved him more than any other man I had ever known. I wanted to be his wife, and I was willing to take a chance that he had changed.

When I told Dennis I was accepting his proposal, he was thrilled. He gathered me up in his arms and swung me around. "You won't regret this," he said. "I promise I'll do everything in my power to make you happy."

We made love then, and it was more intense and urgent than ever before. Afterwards, we clung to each other happily. It was then that I knew I had made the right decision about my life.

We picked out rings the next day, and were married two months later. Everything had been wonderful between us. I had honestly thought I had the perfect marriage until I had overheard Dennis on the phone this morning. He had been making plans for Saturday night!

Janet rolled her chair over to my desk. "Have you calmed down yet, Mary?" she asked.

I smiled bitterly. "You mean, am I going to go home and kill him?" I asked. "No, I've got a better idea. I'm going to cheat on him. Tonight."

Janet's eyes widened in horror. "Tonight?" she repeated in shock. "What do you mean? Are you going to some bar and pick up…"

"Don't be silly," I interrupted, making a face. "I don't want to end up dead! I'm going to sleep with Peter Williams up in accounting. He's asked me out a dozen times this past year. Tonight's his lucky night."

"You can't be serious!" Janet whispered in shock. "That's absolutely crazy! You can't do that."

"Yes, I can," I said calmly. "And I'm going to. Then, I'm going to go home and tell Dennis exactly what I've done. Then he'll know exactly how it feels when someone cheats!"

"This is nuts!" she said. "What about Peter? You'd just be using him!"

I laughed. "Like he'd care!" I exclaimed. "Do you honestly think he's interested in me as a person? He just wants some action. And he's going to get it tonight."

She rolled her eyes. "This has to be the most ridiculous idea I've ever heard," she replied, shaking her head. "And what do you get out of this, Mary? You're mad at Dennis, but you don't care at all about Peter. What good is it going to do you to just have meaningless sex with someone?"

I narrowed my eyes. "I'll get satisfaction," I said evenly. "Dennis told me that Linda meant nothing to him. Now, I can tell him I know what it feels like to have sex with someone who means nothing to me."

Janet laughed. "You know, in a very weird way, that makes sense," she said at last. "I know it's crazy, but I can see your point."

I felt absolutely cold inside as I dialed Peter's number. Within five minutes, he had agreed to meet me after work for drinks.

"Be careful, Mary," Janet warned me, going back to work. "This is a dangerous game you're playing."

Despite my confident tone, I was having serious doubts about my plan. Peter was attractive enough, but I wasn't fooling myself into thinking he really cared about me. He wanted sex, and that was it. But, could I really go through with this?

Just as I was about to call Peter to cancel, however, I thought about Dennis making love to another woman. I could picture the two of them, writhing and sweating. For one moment, I thought I might actually throw up.

"No, I have to do this!" I told myself fiercely. "Dennis can't get away with doing this to me again!"

At the end of the day, I said a hasty goodbye to Janet. I was nervous enough about what I was doing without hearing another lecture from her.

Peter was already waiting at the bar where we'd agreed to meet. I slipped in beside him and ordered a strong drink. When it came, I drank it quickly and ordered another just as fast. Peter smiled at me, and reached for my hand.

"I was surprised that you called," he began softly. "Surprised, but happy."

I hadn't eaten lunch, and the effect of the alcohol was starting to kick in. "I'm glad you feel that way," I said, sitting back. "I think it's about time we got together."

He almost choked on his drink. "Are...are you saying what I think you are?" he asked. "You want us to be together?"

I nodded. "Look, it's probably not for the best of reasons," I said. "But I want to make love to you. We can sit here and have drinks, or we can go to your place and just do it."

He frowned slightly. "Mary, this doesn't sound like you," he answered. "I mean, I want you, but not if you really don't want to."

I swallowed the rest of my second drink. "I said I wanted to," I repeated firmly. "Now, it's up to you. Do you want to make love to me?"

He hesitated for just a fraction of a second. "Sure," he answered finally. "Let's get out of here."

I followed Peter in my own car. When we got to his place, I asked for another drink. He fixed us both one, then sat down on the couch beside me. "We can just sit here and talk if you want," he said. "We don't have to do anything else."

I almost laughed out loud. Peter had been flirting with me, and making suggestive remarks for months. Now, when I was right here in his apartment, ready to have sex, he wanted to talk!

I didn't laugh, though. I needed him for revenge. "No talking," I said. "Let's go into the bedroom."

I didn't waste any time. I stripped off my clothes and climbed onto the bed. Peter seemed surprised, but he quickly followed suit. When he kissed me, I responded easily to the feel of his mouth on mine, and the touch of his strong hands.

I wasn't in love with him by any stretch of the imagination, but I couldn't deny that he was making me feel good. His hands caressed my bare breasts lightly, and I moaned with pleasure.

"Mary, you're so beautiful," he said, kissing my neck. "Even better than I imagined."

I was more than a little drunk, and that helped me ignore the little voice inside of my head that was telling me this was so very wrong. It wasn't just that I was breaking my marriage vows – my body was betraying Dennis as well. I wanted Peter!

Peter was a good lover, brining me quickly to climax, then himself. It was only afterwards that I realized what I had done. I pushed Peter away and started crying. Instantly, Peter gathered me back in his arms, and held me close.

"Mary, what's wrong?" he asked, worried. "I thought you wanted this. You said you did."

"I did," I said miserably. "But I told you it was for all the wrong reasons. I only did this to get back at Dennis for cheating on me. Now, I feel awful about what I did."

Peter wasn't angry. "It was the wrong reason," he agreed. "You're not like that, Mary. You're going to feel worse than he ever did."

"I'm sorry, Peter," I said sincerely. "It wasn't very nice of me to do this to you, either."

He smiled kindly. "I'm not complaining," he said gently. "I wanted this, too. You'd be very easy to fall in love with. If you ever want to get even with your husband again, just call me."

I kissed him, and got out of bed. I was going home to confront Dennis and tell him what had happened, but I didn't feel very good about it. What I had done was just as bad as his cheating on me. Two wrongs definitely didn't make a right. I hadn't solved anything.

When I walked in the door, Dennis looked relieved. "I was starting to worry about you," he said. "I was just about to start calling your friends."

I drew a deep breath. "Speaking of phone calls," I began coldly. "I heard you on the phone this morning making plans for this weekend."

He frowned. "You heard that?" he asked unhappily. "Well, that ruins everything!"

"Ruins everything?" I repeated, shocked. "What do you mean?"

"I was making reservations for our anniversary celebration," he said. "I was going to take you to that new bed-and-breakfast inn that just opened in Prairie City."

For one moment, I thought I might actually faint. Dennis hadn't been making plans with his girlfriend at all! In fact, he had only been thinking of me, and of our marriage. I had completely forgotten our anniversary!

"You were?" I managed weakly.

"Well, we can still go," he said matter-of-factly. "I just wanted it to be a surprise for you."

"Oh, it was," I said honestly. "I'm sorry I spoiled it."

"Why were you late?" he asked curiously. "Extra work at the office?"

"I stopped off for a drink with the girls," I lied quickly. "I'm sorry. I didn't think to call you. I didn't know I'd be so late."

"That's okay," he said. "I was just starting to make spaghetti for dinner. Hope you're hungry."

The last thing in the world I wanted was to eat dinner! "Sounds good," I said. "I'll just take a quick bath before dinner."

Once I'd shut the bathroom door, I burst into tears. I had done the worst thing in the world to my husband, and then lied about it! But how could I tell him the truth? It would ruin everything!

I managed to stop crying, and I ran the bath as hot as I could stand it. I wanted to scrub away every trace of Peter. Of course, I knew that wasn't really possible. The guilt was going to stay with me for a lifetime.

37

I probably should have confessed what I did. A good marriage depends on honesty and trust. But I chose the coward's way out. The shame I feel every day is my punishment, and I intend to do everything I can to make it up to Dennis.

I learned a valuable lesson that night, and I know now that it's wrong to want revenge, especially on someone you love. Janet tried to warn me, but I wouldn't listen. I suppose it's something I had to discover for myself.

I'm lucky to have been given a second chance in my marriage. Maybe I don't deserve it, but I'm going to take it!

THE END

SEX PRISONER
It's the only way to satisfy my needs

A weary glance at the illuminated dial of my clock radio showed me that it was a little after midnight when my husband called out for me.

Ordinarily, I didn't make it to the couch in the parlor where I slept before Carey had called me back to his hospital bed in the room that we'd once shared. It was a small breach in our routine, but it was enough to keep me from closing my eyes.

"I'm coming, I'm coming," I said.

I hesitated in Carey's doorway, telling myself that I mustn't think about how many trips I'd already made to his bedside since supper when Robert, his aide, had left for the night. I didn't want to think of how many trips I would make before breakfast, when Robert would return, so I forced a smile to my face.

There was a time when I'd fantasized about sex. After a stroke had left my much-older husband helpless, though, all I fantasized about was a good night's sleep.

"Would you like some water?" I asked in a low voice, even though there was no one else in the house to disturb. I could have yelled, and I could have screamed in frustration, and no one would have heard me. It was true that only a driveway separated us from our neighbors, the Johnsons, but it might as well have been the Grand Canyon.

"Yes, Alysha, I'd like some water, please. My throat's so dry. And, hon, while you're out there—"

Mentally, I completed his sentence. He was going to tell me to make sure I locked the back door.

"Make sure that you lock the back door," he said.

A few moments later, I was filling a pitcher at the kitchen sink when I heard the Johnsons' dog bark. It was a sound that I normally wouldn't have noticed in the past, but I knew that now, Carey would fuss about it. Since the stroke, outside noises irritated him to no end, which was part of the reason that the house had to be sealed at all times. Robert had tried every way that he could to get Carey to allow a little sunlight and fresh air in, but it was a lost cause.

I knew that the back door was bolted against any intruders, but I checked it, anyway.

When I went back into his room, Carey sipped a little water as the breathing tube in his neck bobbed up and down. I knew that pneumonia was the real intruder in our lives. Carey wasn't able to cough forcefully and he was in constant danger of drowning in his own lung secretions. Several times a day, Robert would snake a suction catheter down the tube. At night, I did it.

With a tissue, I wiped away the fat beads of sweat which dotted Carey's face. His skin was cool, but his body's ability to regulate its temperature—his internal thermostat—had gone haywire. Still, the gesture reminded me of how I'd once traced the contours of his handsome face with my fingers after we'd made love. I'd gone from being my husband's trophy wife to being his nursemaid.

"What do you think about changing your pillowcase, baby?" I asked gently.

It had to be his idea. So intense was his need to be independent, to control his confined world now, as he'd once controlled the English department of a major university, that something as simple as changing his pillowcase could provoke a power struggle.

"Leave it alone," Carey snapped. "Why is that dog making such a racket? What's the matter with that dog?"

I knew that the only thing I could do when he was peevish was to distract him.

"You need a haircut," I said, to get him off the subject. I couldn't hear the dog any longer, but Carey's ears seemed to hear the grass grow.

"A haircut? What for?" he grumbled. "Nobody sees me, except for you and Robert."

Sadly, it was true. The once-magnetic leader in the academic community had been largely forgotten by his peers. His family's attention was grudging at best. His two adult daughters put on a good performance. Nell and Carlotta showed up whenever the demands of their busy, successful lives allowed. I dreaded their visits. They'd been hateful to me before Carey's stroke, and now that he couldn't defend me, they were downright evil.

Everyone had cautioned me against marrying a man three times my age. Of course, I'd been too headstrong and too much in love to heed anything except the voice of my heart. Professor Carey Nelson had been the god of my idolatry and I'd wanted him the way I wanted air to breathe and food to eat. I was nineteen and he was fifty-seven when we met. In my opinion, brothers my own age were merely silly schoolboys.

I was saving myself for Superman.

When I first laid eyes on Carey he was Superman, rugged and virile. His voice rolled like thunder across the enormous lecture hall where, over the heads of two hundred other students, he and I connected in a shower of sparks. Of course, it was against university policy for a faculty member to date a student, much less sleep with one. The illicit nature of our relationship made it an adventure.

That's all it would have remained, had it not been for a threat from the university administration to take disciplinary action against Carey.

"Just a bunch of narrow-minded old coots, all jealous because I've found the fountain of youth!" he bragged.

"Daddy's little mid-life crisis," was what his daughters called me.

Only six weeks after we'd met, to thumb our noses at the establishment, Carey and I had recklessly eloped to Las Vegas. Nell's response to her father's phone call from the wedding chapel had turned out to be prophetic, after all that had happened since.

"Well, Daddy, tell Alysha that if she marries in haste, she'll repent at leisure," she'd said.

She'd been so right. Allowed to run a natural course, our fiery passion would have burned itself out. At twenty-five, I would have been looking back on my first love affair with tenderness instead of pity.

"Are you uncomfortable, Carey? Do you want a sleeping pill?" I asked.

"Can't you see that I'm sick of lying in the same position?" Carey snarled, in the sarcastic tone that had become his power over me. Isolated from other people, and overwhelmed with responsibility, I longed for my husband's approval now more than ever, but nothing I did pleased him.

We could have well afforded around-the-clock professional nurses, but when Carey became an invalid, I assumed most of his care myself. I felt that it was my duty, but I also wanted to prove to his resentful daughters that I took my marriage vows seriously. Though Carey had known about—and ignored—his high blood pressure for years, they blamed me for his stroke. Certainly, they didn't appreciate my devotion.

I helped Carey turn onto his side, then left his room to return to my lonely couch. I was just about to close my eyes when he called to me again.

"Aren't you going to change my pillowcase?" he asked.

It was going to be another long night, I thought.

Robert Steele was the one bright spot in my life. Even Carey, as sour as he'd become, couldn't resist Robert's happy smile and warm personality. I had no family, and all my friends had drifted away. Robert was often the only person, besides Carey, that I spoke to for days at a time.

"Girl, you need a vacation," Robert teased, his dark eyes dancing with mischief.

That was a regular routine with us, our private joke. My comeback was always the same.

"Where you going to take me?" I'd ask.

"Hawaii!" was always his quick response . . . or Paris, or the North Pole. It didn't matter, really. "Vacation" was our word for the coffee breaks that we enjoyed while Carey took his afternoon naps. Our destination was always the same: the kitchen.

When Robert first came to work for us he'd tried to get me to sit down so that he could serve me. He pretended to be a bumbling waiter and did all kinds of funny stuff. Even though I laughed at his antics, I felt so nervous—and so bad about enjoying myself when poor Carey couldn't—that Robert finally gave up and let me take care of him.

"Alysha, your self-esteem is so low that I'm surprised you don't say you're sorry to the air, for breathing it," he once commented.

Guilty as charged. I constantly apologized and I constantly criticized myself. Always thinking of me last, or not at all, had eaten away at my confidence and pride. It was like sinking into quicksand, without a branch or a hand to grab onto.

Where was the bold, high-spirited young sister I'd been before sacrifice became my life? After Carey and I married, I'd felt too grown-up for school, so I dropped out. I'd had a job I enjoyed in a small art gallery, but I gave it up when Carey was stricken.

Robert understood my situation and we often discussed it.

"Alysha, you need to get out of the house every now and then. What's with his daughters? Why can't one of them come around some evening to give you a break?"

I put on a brave front. "We don't want any favors from those two heifers! Carey and I are fine. We like being independent. We don't need them."

Robert sighed. "Alysha, this is no life for you. You're a young woman. You need to go back to school and to finish your education. Dr. Nelson, he's a fine, distinguished man and all, but he's not doing right. I see how he picks at you. It's like he's got to belittle you, keep you down, so you won't leave him."

That kind of talk made me defensive. "You didn't know Carey before his illness, Robert. The sick man you see in that hospital bed is not the real Carey, not the Carey who risked everything to make me his wife. He defied the university, and he defied his own family, for my sake. I love him. Love means putting the others person's welfare ahead of your own."

I'd never known a man as sympathetic as Robert. He sensed my pain and he didn't want to offend me.

"You're a good wife, Alysha, a good person. You honor your

commitments. I only hope Dr. Nelson realizes how fortunate he is to have your loyalty."

It was a wonderful compliment, but I didn't deserve it. Robert couldn't know my secret. He couldn't know that late at night, when my longing for release became a hunger that couldn't be ignored, I imagined his hands—not my poor husband's—stroking my body. Robert's lips, not Carey's, were the ones that I craved. It was Robert's name I cried out in the darkness.

One of the things most women my age took for granted was the future, but my world was so restricted, my days so monotonous, that I'd lost hope. I was trapped. It seemed my morale couldn't sink any lower, but I was wrong.

Robert and I were having one of our "vacations" one day when I noticed that he seemed quieter than usual. With the numb disbelief you feel between a blow and the pain, I received the news that he would be leaving in the fall to complete his education. For me, it was a sentence of death.

He couldn't meet my eyes and addressed his coffee cup as he spoke the words that shattered my world.

"I've been accepted into a physician's assistant program. It's a pretty tough course. It'll take five years to get my degree, but it's what I've always wanted," he told me earnestly.

My brave front crumbled as a hard lump in my throat dissolved; losing Robert, my only ally, was too much. I squeezed my eyes shut to hold back my grief, but like a raging river, my tears burst and I sobbed loudly.

He got up from the table and tried to comfort me. "Alysha, don't—"

I pushed him away and ran out of the kitchen and down the hall. I threw myself down on the couch and covered my face with a pillow. So great was my distress that I actually sank my teeth into it to keep from screaming.

Robert sat by my side, cooing my name, and murmuring reassurance.

"It's okay, baby. It's going to be okay," he whispered.

He took me into his strong arms and held me until I was calm. I clung to him.

"Oh, Robert, don't leave. You're the only person in the world who understands the hell I'm going through. I don't want to be alone!"

His lips brushed my forehead. "It's going to be all right, Alysha. We're going to come up with a plan, I promise. We're going to fix things. I'm not leaving for two months. Before I leave, you're going to have your life back, girl."

I nuzzled his neck. "Just hold me, Robert. I can't think beyond this moment. Hold me—kiss me," I pleaded.

He didn't hesitate. Our lips met in mutual desire and I knew at once that he'd been wanting me as much as I'd been wanting him. We pulled off our clothes and he explored my body with his hands and tongue.

"I hate the way he treats you, Alysha. You're beautiful," he told me.

I shook my head as I arched my back to accept his manhood. I gasped and began to match at his movements, moaning my pleasure at our shared rhythm.

"You really are beautiful," he panted. "I've dreamt about this moment."

His delicate hands ran up and down my body until I couldn't control the ferocious screams that came out of my mouth. I grabbed the pillow underneath my head as Robert ran his soft hands along my hardened peaks. Realizing my husband was in the next room, I worked hard to stifle the moans that rose in the pit of my throat. All words were replaced by the sweet sound of lovemaking. Over and over again, my body shuddered as Robert delivered kisses and caresses I hadn't felt in months.

I was dazed as his love increased and he eased his manhood into me gently. Sweat poured off his face as we both created or own rhythms. Delicately, he handled my body like a scientist handling a top secret project. Robert knew how to make me climax uncontrollably. Passion formed in my throat while I hollered for more. But I knew my body wouldn't be able to take the grips of pleasure much longer.

My lips moved, silently forming the words to match his thrusts, until, at the shattering moment of ecstasy, I screamed the words aloud. I wanted Robert to stay with me. His own sweet climax met mine as his body shuddered on top of me. I clung to his strong arms and taut torso. We laid in each other's arms for what seemed like days before we drifted into light slumber.

Robert insisted that the first thing I needed to do to regain my self-esteem was to stand up to Carey's bossy family. He told me that the way they used and abused me was disgraceful. Nell, a high-flying real estate developer, rarely checked on her father in person. She said that she couldn't bear to see her father in that condition so, even though she lived just a short distance away, she called, rather than visited.

"Alysha, I'm right in the middle of a crisis," was how she frantically began every phone conversation. Nell always seemed to be on the brink of some disaster that kept her from seeing her father. "Now, what did the doctor say about the pressure sore on Daddy's heel? If you changed Daddy's position more often, he wouldn't have any problem with his skin. Are you massaging Daddy's heels? Are you giving Daddy his vitamins? Is Daddy getting the kind of food he likes? Nutrition is so important." Her barrage of questions was endless.

Nell sounded put out, having to ask all those exhausting questions, but she let it be known that no amount of effort was too much to make sure that her daddy was getting taken care of properly—by somebody else.

Carlotta was much more of an ordeal. Not only did she show up in person, she'd bring along her mother—Carey's ex-wife, Olivia. When the two of them arrived, I was crowded out of my own home.

Olivia and Carey had been history years before I'd ever appeared on the scene, but you'd have thought that I'd broken up their marriage, the way she stared daggers at me.

Carlotta was a high school principle and she treated me like one of her duller students.

"Alysha, my mother and I need to talk to Dr. Nelson in private, if you'll kindly step out of the room. We'll call you when we need you," Carlotta harped.

She always referred to her father as "Dr. Nelson" in my presence, a subtle way of putting me in my place. Of course, it made me furious to be dismissed. There was nothing I could do about it, though, because Carey refused to intervene on my behalf.

The bathroom attached to our bedroom also had an entrance from the hallway. Curious to know what they were talking about, I slipped in there to eavesdrop.

"What'd you expect when you robbed the cradle?" Olivia's spiteful voice came through the locked door, loud and unmistakable.

Carlotta cleared her throat. "Don't start that now, Mama. We have business here. Daddy, you need to sign these transfer forms to move that account we want to hide."

I knew that Carlotta managed her father's investments. Carey had money in all kinds of stocks and bonds. The subject of finances was way over my head. I couldn't make my checkbook balance, but the fact that they were talking about hiding an account alerted me to the fact that something underhanded was going on.

"Daddy, I know that it upsets you, but we need to talk about giving me power of attorney so I can have complete control of your assets in case anything should happen."

Carey's voice cracked like a whip. "Can't wait to get your greedy paws on my money, can you, baby girl? Well, I'm not incompetent. There's nothing wrong with my mind!" He began to wheeze and choke.

"Now, see what you've done?" Olivia accused her daughter.

"That vixen he married gave him the first stroke, and you'll give him a second one if you're not careful!"

Carlotta began to scream. "Alysha! Alysha, hurry up, Daddy's having an attack!" She always pushed the panic button when Carey had a simple coughing spasm.

Robert was horrified when I confided all this to him. Our "vacations" were now spent on the couch. We made love every day, but the holding and the cuddling afterward meant more to me than the sex.

I had only a vague idea of what having power of attorney might mean.

"It's means that Carlotta could legally sign Dr. Nelson's name to anything," Robert explained. "She could cut you off without a penny!"

I couldn't believe it. "That's impossible, Robert—I'm his wife. He changed his will in my favor. I'm entitled to inherit his estate."

Robert smoothed my hair. "I'm not talking about when he's dead, Alysha—that could be years from now. The minute that Carlotta can sign his name, she can transfer everything he owns into her own name. There could be nothing left in his estate by the time you inherit it. You heard that they're already starting to hide his accounts."

Money had been the last thing on my mind when I'd impulsively eloped with Carey. My parents and older siblings had been killed in a house fire when I was an infant and I had been raised by a distant, cold-hearted cousin. Money couldn't buy the kind of protection that I'd always wanted from a loved one.

Suddenly, my husband, who'd vowed to forsake all others, was willing to help Carlotta stab me in the back! I just assumed loyalty to a spouse went both ways in a marriage. My illusions were shattered.

It was a big step when I took hold of my courage to let Carey know that I was aware of Carlotta's crafty plan to do me out of what was legally mine. I expected him to twist things around with his silver tongue, to use my own words against me, to make me feel foolish and at fault. Instead, he readily admitted everything.

"Alysha, you have to understand my precarious position. I can't afford to alienate my daughters. I may be dependent on them someday soon."

I took his hand. "You'll never be dependent on them, honey. You have me."

When Carey smiled tenderly I saw the ghost of the man I'd adored.

"Alysha, you won't be here much longer. I know about you and Robert. I'm crippled, but I'm not blind or deaf."

Confronted so frankly with my wrongdoing, I went hot with

46

shame. There was no reproach in Carey's eyes, and yet, even so, I was mortified, and begged his forgiveness.

"Don't go there, baby," he said softly. "I can't blame you for being young. I knew I was running out of time when we met, Alysha. A medical test told me that my arteries were blocked. I refused to follow what the doctors prescribed. I always did things my way and I decided that I didn't care about the consequences. That was my choice, Alysha. I should never have dragged you into it."

Tears were streaming down my cheeks. "I've been so lonely all my life. When I was a little girl, all I wanted was a family. I wanted to belong to you, Carey. I wanted to be your wife. That was my choice. I'll never, ever leave you."

He sighed sadly. "Well, Alysha, one of these days neither one of us is going to have a choice." His words stayed in my head for days.

Like a child playing make-believe, I lived in the moment and refused to deal with the reality of Robert leaving. In his gentle way, he tried to prepare me for September, when he would be gone, but I couldn't stand the slightest hint along those lines.

When he mentioned a going-away party, I stared at him blankly.

"A party?" I repeated.

He playfully tweaked my nose. "A going-away party. Some friends are giving me a party Saturday night. Nothing fancy—just beer and a bonfire down on the beach."

I was peeling vegetables at the kitchen sink. The onions had already brought tears to my eyes. With a pang, I realized that Robert had a whole life, a life that I knew nothing about. He had friends and family that I'd probably never meet.

"That's nice," I said.

He laughed. "I want you to come."

If he'd have said, "I want you to fly around the room," I couldn't have been more astounded.

"Robert, you know that's impossible. I can't leave Carey alone."

Robert gave me a frisky little swat on the backside.

"Of course not. Get one of your ugly stepdaughters to baby-sit, Mrs. Cinderella."

I tossed a handful of carrot curls into his face. "Oh, sure, like they'd do me a favor."

Robert grabbed the faucet hose attachment and threatened to spray me.

"You don't put it to them as a favor, you get one of them over here, tell her that you'll see her later, and walk out the door." He aimed a blast of water at the front of my T-shirt.

Squealing with glee, I tried to wrestle the hose away from him and we both ended up soaked.

Robert gave me encouragement all week. I was certain that I wouldn't be able to go through with it, but late Saturday afternoon, I called Carlotta.

"Your father wants you to come over this evening." I couldn't resist adding my next remark. "He's willing to discuss some kind of papers you want him to sign."

That worked like a charm.

I didn't need a mirror to tell me how cute I looked, with my hair just right, when Carlotta and her mother arrived. It had been so long since I'd fussed over my appearance. That night was special, and I wanted to make myself special for Robert.

Carlotta did a double take when she saw the figure-hugging silk slip dress I'd never worn before—it'd hung in my closet for three years with the price tag still on it.

Olivia's eyes narrowed. "You look like a hooker."

Keep moving, I thought. Don't give them an opening.

I had the satisfaction of seeing their mouths drop open in unison when I breezed out the door.

"I have my cell phone if there's a problem. Be back around midnight!" I called over my shoulder, and then ran out into the night—free at last!

I soon learned that high-heeled sandals were no good for walking in sand. I kicked mine off soon after we joined Robert's friends on the beach. My head was held high. The simple act of greeting new people seemed like liberation. My heart sang with such joy over my freedom, I was drunk without taking a single drink!

I shocked Robert by being the belle of the ball. He'd worried that I wouldn't be able to enjoy myself. He was certainly wrong! I knew that the memory of that night was going to have to sustain me for a long time after he departed for college, so I'd decided to enjoy each and every moment for all it was worth.

My cell phone began to go off five minutes after I'd gotten to the beach. It was an angry Carlotta, of course.

"Alysha, who do you think you are?" she began.

Robert correctly interpreted the grimace on my face. Before I could protest, he snatched the phone out of my hands and shut it off. Then, he shoved it into his own pocket.

"Robert, what if there's an emergency?" I asked.

"I guess they'll have to deal with it," he answered easily.

Caught up in the music and laughter, I didn't give it another thought and, as the night wore on, it was if I'd hit the rewind button on my life. I was young again—carefree and happy.

When the moon came out, Robert and I left the bonfire and walked along the shore, holding hands. We stopped to kiss deeply.

Our lips parted with a soft, sexy sound, but I couldn't bring myself to open my eyes.

"Oh, Robert, if only this could last forever," I whispered.

He nibbled my earlobe, sending a shiver through my core.

"It can, Alysha. It can, if you'll come with me."

"I won't leave Carey, not as long as he needs me," I told him, my eyes still closed.

"I need you," Robert whispered urgently. His hands traveled down my back to caress me. "We could have a life together—a future."

I opened my eyes to feast on the sight of his beloved face. "It's not the same kind of need. I have an obligation to my husband."

"You know, Alysha, in ancient Egypt the wives of the pharaohs were expected to join him in death. That was their idea of an obligation."

"Take me home, Robert," I demanded suddenly, fighting off tears.

After I located my sandals, we left the party without saying good-bye to anyone and drove home in silence. What was there to say? Yes, losing Robert would be torment, but I'd had no right to his love in the first place. I was, after all, a married woman.

Robert pulled up at the curb in front of my house and we sat there, neither one of us ready to end our bittersweet first—and last—date. I wanted to tell him how much he meant to me. The words came to my lips just as I noticed that there was a big dog sitting on my porch. Then, the front door opened and a woman stepped out.

Carlotta's car was still parked in our driveway, but it wasn't Carlotta or her mother who followed the dog down the walk. It was our neighbor, Mrs. Johnson. Instinctively, I knew that something awful had taken place.

"Oh, Mrs. Nelson," she said breathlessly, in a tone of relief. "I'm not used to such excitement. We tried calling you. The ambulance just left for the emergency room—"

It was my worst fear come true. I gave an anguished cry. Robert hit the gas pedal and we peeled away with a squeal of tires. I tried to pray as Robert raced the short distance to the nearest hospital, but all that would come out was, "Oh, God, please." I suspected the worst had happened.

His car hadn't even slowed to a stop at the emergency room entrance when I jumped out of the passenger side. I twisted my ankle badly, but I didn't feel the pain as I hobbled through the automatic doors into the brightly lit waiting area. I limped straight to the reception desk and demanded to see my husband.

The nurse on duty was accustomed to dealing with distraught people. She coolly checked a list.

"Yes, we have a Nelson here. Carey was brought in a little while ago. His chart indicates syncope was the reason he was brought here."

Robert came up behind me with a wheelchair and forced me to sit down. He gave my name to the nurse and we waited for several hours to have my ankle checked. He explained that syncope meant that my husband had fainted.

When I got home, Carey relished telling me what happened.

"Got herself all agitated and upset because I had a coughing spasm. Olivia and Carlotta ran around the house screaming and panicking. By the time they called 911, I must have passed out."

The twinkle in Carey's eye told me that he'd enjoyed the commotion enormously. Then he said something so unexpected, so cruel, that it stunned me.

"Alysha, I've allowed Carlotta to take charge of my finances because I intend to file for divorce. If you go along with us and agree to make this easy, you'll get a generous settlement. Enough to return to school and live comfortably. I want you out of what's left of my life."

I gasped. "But why, Carey-because of Robert?"

Suddenly, tears sparkled in his eyes. "Because I love you. Love means putting the other person's welfare ahead of your own."

It wasn't easy. At first, I was in a fog of grief. I'd always been overly emotional, exaggerating even trivial hurts. Of course, what I was going through was no trivial hurt—I'd had the rug pulled out from under me. Thankfully, Robert was there to cushion my fall. When he left for school, I left with him.

Carey had wanted an unsophisticated girl who would admire him without question. I'd wanted a strong man, my own Superman, to protect me. Any marriage based on such shortsighted needs was doomed. We couldn't have gone on as we were, but I didn't know how to break free. People changed as they were challenged. I soon realized that it was Carey, not Robert, who had given me my life back.

With Robert as my partner, I've found a comfortable balance between my desire for intimacy and security and my suppressed desire for growth. Like a butterfly, my self-esteem has emerged from the cocoon I'd spun around it.

Thanks to the large settlement I accepted from Carey, I completed college with honors. Going on to medical school was now my dream, but it's a dream I had happily put on hold until the baby Robert and I was expecting, was born.

I suppose Carlotta thought she was doing the decent thing when she sent me a copy of her father's obituary. I was in the last month of pregnancy and my belly was huge with Robert, Jr. I wept softly as I read the glowing newspaper tributes to Dr. Carey Nelson.

50

Carey had granted me the new life I was entitled to. My marriage to Robert was one of the greatest things in my life. And I was glad that love had finally entered my once sheltered life.

THE END

PAINFUL REGRET
Why Did I Marry Him?

I was still breathing heavily when David rolled off my naked body. "We can't keep doing this," I said to him. "This has to be the last time. Absolutely the last time."

David laughed. "Sarey, you say the same thing every time," he replied, lighting up a cigarette and taking a long drag. "And every time I remind you that the sex between us is incredible. Are you honestly telling me you wouldn't miss our afternoons together if we stopped seeing each other?"

I sighed. "Of course I would," I replied unhappily. "But what if Michael finds out about us? Or your wife does? What would we do then?"

"That's why we're so careful," he replied casually. "Look, I'm not crazy about cheating on Debra, but what we have going on is pretty special, too. Admit it. You don't have sex like this with Michael, do you? You never have. He doesn't make you moan and scream with pleasure the way I do."

"No, he doesn't," I admitted. "But…"

"But you're feeling guilty," he finished for me. "You should feel guilty. We're cheating on the people we're married to. It's wrong and immoral and we both know it. It also makes the sex more exciting."

I didn't know if it was the sneaking around behind Michael's back or that David was simply a wonderful lover, but I couldn't seem to think about anything else but being with him. When we weren't together, I daydreamed about our next lovemaking session. So far, Michael didn't seem to suspect a thing about my relationship with David, but how long could that last?

David began tracing circles around my nipples with his tongue. His hands roamed possessively up and down my eager body. "We've got time to make love again," he whispered suggestively. "Come on, it's early. I need you."

"I…I can't," I managed to gasp. "I have to pick up Asha at the bus stop in half an hour. Plus, if I don't get to the grocery store pretty soon, Michael is going to wonder what I do after work."

David laughed. "Just tell him you're having incredible sex with an accountant from the office," he teased. "And that you'd rather be in bed with him than at the grocery store, picking out cereal and juice boxes for the kids."

"Very funny!" I snapped impatiently. "If Michael found out

about this, it would kill him. He loves me and trusts me. He's given me everything I ever asked for. He would never understand my having an affair!"

I was angry with David, but I was really furious with myself. Michael trusted me and I was cheating on him with another man! There was no excuse for it, except that I couldn't seem to stop myself.

"Look, baby, I'm sorry," David said, pulling me back down beside him on the bed. "But you need to face the facts. You don't love your husband. Hell, he's almost twice your age! Sure, he's a nice guy, but you don't love him. You married him so he could be a father to Asha and Jason."

I felt tears well up in my eyes at the thought. "And he's been so good to them," I whispered. "And to me."

David's tone grew gentle. "Yes, he has," he replied. "He sounds like a great guy. But maybe he's not the husband you need."

David kissed me then, and I felt the same intense desire I always felt when David was touching me. "Okay," I said, finally. "But we have to be fast."

David knew right where to touch me with his hands and mouth so that I felt like I would die if he didn't make love to me right away! I wanted him inside of me immediately and I knew that it would only be moments before we both climaxed. Sex was good every time between us and had been since the very beginning.

It was only on the way home that I felt my head begin to clear. I was too late to pick up Asha at the bus stop, so I could only hurry home with some excuse about working extra hours at the insurance firm.

Asha was already eating a snack when I walked in the door. "Hi, Mommy," she said happily. "I let myself in the back door again."

"Oh, honey, I'm sorry," I apologized quickly. "There was just so much work at the office, I couldn't get away."

She frowned slightly. "I thought you were only working in the mornings, Mommy," she said. "You've had to work late a lot."

"Well, it should quiet down soon," I lied. "My boss promised me that in a few weeks, I shouldn't have to work any extra hours at all."

"Good," she said, smiling up at me. "I miss having you pick me up at the bus stop after school. And I miss your cookies and brownies. You never have time to bake anymore."

"I know," I said, trying to sound cheerful. "I'm sorry about that. Why don't you and I run to the grocery store while your brother is still at soccer practice?"

"Okay," she agreed.

I breathed a sigh of relief that Asha was such an agreeable child. Of course, she was almost 10, and probably old enough to be left on her own, but that's not the way I wanted her raised. As much as I hated to admit it to myself, she and her brother, Jason, was the main reason I had married Michael.

I had been 15 when I got pregnant with Jason. I was young and stupid, and thought my boyfriend, Eddie, would stick by me. I had been naïve enough to think he might even want a baby. I had honestly expected a marriage proposal. Instead, he had dumped me so fast it had made my head spin.

My parents were furious with me, but they let me stay at home and I even went back to high school after Jason was born. But then I met Patrick, and made the same mistake all over again. Asha was his daughter, and he cared even less than Eddie had cared about Jason. I suppose it was kind of amazing how I managed to meet and fall in love with two such complete jerks!

So, at 17, I had two children, no fathers for them and no real future. That's when Michael had walked into my life. He was a friend of my aunt's and I had known him casually for years.

I had always thought he was good-looking in a way, but I had never thought of him as boyfriend material. For one thing, he was closer to my father's age than mine. And I had always liked men with a dangerous edge. Michael was simply a really nice guy.

One day, however, he asked if he could take Asha, Jason and me out for ice cream. "I like kids," he said, almost shyly. "But, unfortunately, I got divorced before I had any of my own. I'd like to buy your kids a treat."

"That would be nice," I answered. "The kids love ice cream. So do I."

I had a better time with him than I expected. Michael was so good with the kids, and they absolutely adored him. While I ate my double-chocolate chip ice cream cone, Michael talked about his first marriage.

"Tina was a career girl from the very beginning, and I knew that," he said. "She loved her job at the hospital and she was good at it. She kept getting promotions and making more money. We talked about having children and a real family home – someday.

"I tried to give her as much freedom as she needed," he continued sadly. "I didn't question the long hours or the travel. But, finally, I realized she didn't really want a family and a home. I didn't blame her for not loving me enough to want a family with me. But it still hurt."

I smiled at him. "I guess my story is just the opposite," I said honestly. "I wasn't very smart. I had the children first and then nobody wanted to be my husband."

"It's their loss," he said seriously. "Sarey, you're a very beautiful, smart woman. Any man would be lucky to have you as a wife."

That was the beginning of our relationship. After our ice cream date, Michael started coming around to take us all out for pizza or to the movies. It was Michael who took Asha to the zoo for the first time and signed Jason up for swimming lessons. He became the only father figure they had ever known. And they adored him.

The problem was, we never had a date alone until my 19th birthday. Michael arranged for my parents to baby sit Asha and Jason, then made reservations at one of the nicest restaurants in town. He surprised me by showing up at my doorstep that night with a huge bouquet of red roses. He handed me the flowers and kissed me lightly on the mouth.

"Wear something fancy," he told me. "I wanted to take you someplace nice for your birthday."

While I dressed, I thought about what dating Michael could mean to my life. I wasn't really attracted to him as a boyfriend, but I figured that was probably a good thing. Certainly, the men I had been attracted to in the past had been pretty awful. I didn't have very good judgment when it came to men.

And Michael was so good with my children. I longed to move out of my parents' house and into a place of my own. But with my part-time job at the convenience store, that wasn't going to be possible for a long time. Michael could give me a different kind of life and I knew it.

When I came out, Michael whistled. "You're so very beautiful, Sarey," he said softly. "Happy birthday."

Michael ordered champagne at the restaurant, and lobster. "I've been wanting to go out with you alone for a long time," he began. "I like you a lot, Sarey. You've probably realized I want a serious relationship with you."

"I like you, too," I answered carefully. "And the kids love you."

"Look, I know this might seem strange to you," he said, staring straight at me. "But I'd like us to go steady, if that's the right term for it. I know I'm a lot older than you are, and I've already been married once...."

"I'd like us to be a couple," I interrupted, reaching over to take his hand. "You've been so good to me and the kids."

It wasn't the most romantic beginning to a relationship, but I didn't care. Suddenly, there was a man in my life who really cared about me, and about my children. He treated me with respect and really enjoyed being with me. After two months of dating, I agreed to marry him.

The wedding was small, but I thought it was beautiful. I had the long, white dress I'd always dreamed of, and the wedding cake trimmed with pink sugar roses. It bothered me that I wasn't really in love with my new husband, but I also realized how good my life would be with him.

Obviously, I wasn't a virgin, but Michael wanted to wait until our wedding night to make love to me. "I want it to be special for both of us," he said. "After all, we're going to be together for the rest of our lives."

That night, I put on my new, peach-colored negligee. I was a bit embarrassed as I faced Michael for the first time wearing practically nothing at all. He looked at me with love and devotion.

"I can't believe you're my wife," he whispered. "You're so very lovely. I feel like it's just a dream and I'm going to wake up at any moment."

Michael stood up and kissed me tenderly. Very gently, he stripped the nightgown from my body. Every caress told me how much he loved me and adored my body. He made sure I was completely aroused before he entered me, and I was more than satisfied with his performance in bed.

When Michael made love to me, it felt very safe and comfortable. Deep down, I knew the lovemaking lacked the fire and intensity of my other lovers, but I convinced myself that it didn't matter.

Afterwards, Michael held me tightly. "I love you so much, Sarey," he said fiercely. "I'll do everything I can to make you happy."

The next day, we left for our honeymoon in Hawaii. We spent a week there, making love and relaxing in the sun. It was the first time since I'd given birth to Asha and Jason that I felt completely carefree and happy. I only had to take care of myself: eat when I was hungry and drink pina coladas until I was giddily drunk. I didn't really want to go back home and take over all my responsibilities again.

"Sarey, I'm going to make sure your life is much better from now on," Michael assured me. "The first thing we're going to do is find a big house with a huge backyard for the kids. Then, you're going to stay at home with them and take care of all of us."

I was so excited and grateful by Michael's plan. I wanted nothing more than to provide a stable home for Asha and Jason. They deserved to have a normal childhood like other children.

We bought a nice house in a good neighborhood. The kids thrived in their new school and Jason went out for every athletic team there was. Asha joined the Girl Scouts and dance class and they both did very well in school.

I should have been perfectly happy and contented, but something was missing. I longed for the excitement and passion of being really in love with my husband. When we made love, it was fine, but I longed for more. I wanted to feel fireworks in the pit of my stomach when Michael touched me.

I was bored at home, and I finally decided the answer was a part-time job. A friend of mine suggested I work mornings in an insurance company nearby. "They always need people," she mentioned casually. "The pay is pretty good and you can set your own hours. And, you'd be home when your kids got home from school."

It sounded perfect. I'd be out of the house for a few hours every day and I could make some extra money. I had always enjoyed working with people and this job didn't require a high school diploma.

Michael wasn't so sure. "Sarey, we don't really need the money," he said, frowning. "You don't have to work if you don't want to."

"Michael, we need to start saving for things like braces and college," I pointed out. "Or we could put my salary aside for a really nice vacation with the kids. I mean, there isn't that much to do around the house when you three are gone all day, so I might as well make myself useful."

Finally, reluctantly, Michael agreed. "But, if it gets to be too much, just quit," he told me. "The kids and I need you here."

I loved working. I enjoyed getting up in the morning, putting on nice clothes and meeting new people. I was good at my job, and my boss really liked me. At my three-month performance appraisal, I was given a promotion and raise.

I'd been working there for almost a year, before I met David. He worked in a different part of the building and only came into our office occasionally. The first time I saw him, I was struck by how tall and handsome he was. His skin was a rich, chocolate color and he did indeed look good enough to eat.

He was also an impossible flirt. "Well, hello beautiful," he said, when he met me. "You must be new around here. I know I haven't seen you before. I'd have remembered that face-and that body."

I felt my face burn. "I'm not sure your wife would appreciate you making comments like that," I said, pointing to his wedding ring.

He just laughed. "I don't plan on going home and telling her that I just met the most beautiful woman in the world either," he replied easily. "I know she wouldn't like that."

David stopped by my desk almost every day. Sometimes, he brought me a cup of coffee and a doughnut, other times a flower or a funny card. It was wrong, of course, and I should have stopped it, but I didn't.

Finally, he asked me to go out to lunch. "I shouldn't," I began hesitantly. "It wouldn't be right."

He grinned at me. "It wouldn't be right to eat lunch?" he asked teasingly. "Don't tell me you'd prefer to eat a carton of yogurt and an apple here when I could offer lasagna at Luigi's."

I frowned at him. "Look, you know we've both been, well,

flirting with each other," I replied. "But that's as far as it's gone. If we start having lunch together, people will start to talk."

He shrugged. "So who cares?" he asked. "Come on, Sarey, we like each other. That's a good enough reason to have lunch together. Besides, Luigi's has the best Italian food in town."

We ate lasagna and talked for the entire lunch hour. I liked David, and I was attracted to his strong good looks. I tried to convince myself we could just be friends, but I should have known better. I had been through this all before.

Soon, we were having lunch together all the time. Since I only worked part-time, David would call me at home to talk while Michael and the kids were gone. It was only a matter of time before he kissed me passionately, and suggested we get a motel room for the afternoon.

Looking back, it's easy to see how I could have prevented the whole affair from ever starting. I should have pushed him away after the first kiss, and told him in no uncertain terms I wasn't interested.

But I was interested. When David kissed me, I felt weak with desire. I just knew he would be a good lover and I wanted him. Michael was a wonderful, reliable husband, but I longed for some excitement in my love life.

We agreed to meet at a motel near the office. I was actually trembling when I walked up the stairs and I almost turned around and got back in my car. Then, David came up behind me.

"I wasn't sure you'd show up," he said softly.

"I almost left," I confessed. "I shouldn't be here."

David kissed me then, and I actually felt my knees might buckle. "You should be here," he corrected me. "We both need this."

David had brought champagne, but we didn't even bother pouring a glass. Instead, David ripped off my clothes urgently and made love to me as though we'd invented sex. It was wonderful and crazy, and, afterwards, I was immediately consumed by guilt.

"This can't happen again," I said, even as my body was still cooling down from the intensity of our lovemaking. "I can't do this to Michael."

David responded by kissing me softly. "Sarey, this was good," he answered. "Too good not to repeat. Don't worry about Michael. You still love him and you're not leaving him. What he doesn't know won't hurt him."

I let David convince me that it wouldn't matter. I couldn't resist the feel of his mouth and hands all over my body. Again and again, he made every nerve tingle as he brought me to the peaks of ecstasy.

Later that night, I was torn between feeling guilty and the pleasure of re-living the glorious sex we'd shared. I made Michael a special dinner that night: fried chicken, green bean casserole and cherry pie.

"Wow!" he said in appreciation. "All my favorites. What's the occasion?"

I felt a nervous flutter deep in my stomach. "Oh, nothing," I answered, hoping I sounded casual. "Just wanted to tell you I loved you." That was a terrible thing to say. I had just gotten out of bed with another man and I was telling my husband I loved him! How hypocritical could I possibly be?

Michael beamed at me. "You're terrific," he said. "And this fried chicken looks delicious."

I hated living a lie, but I couldn't stop myself. When I was with Michael, I swore I wouldn't see David again. He was such a good husband and wonderful father. I had a happy, secure home and I didn't want to jeopardize that.

But, then, I would see David again, and remember the last time we'd made love. I wasn't fooling myself. I didn't love David and I didn't want him to leave his wife for me. But I needed the physical love he could give me.

I was like a chocolate addict who constantly has a box of candy on her desk. There was no way I could resist the sweet, delectable treats right in front of me.

Naturally, it couldn't go on that way. As careful as I thought David and I were being, we slipped up. It was the day that Jason hurt his ankle in gym class. The school called me at work and at home, but of course, I wasn't at either place. I was in the hotel room with David.

When I got home, Michael had already taken Jason to the emergency room and been home for an hour when I arrived. I think he could tell just by looking at me where I'd been.

"We need to talk," he said coolly.

As soon as I made sure Jason was all right and didn't need anything, I followed Michael into the bedroom. "I need to know where you were, Sarey," he said, looking straight at me. "And please don't lie to me. I think you owe me the truth."

Even then, I suppose I could have made up some story about lunch with another friend or shopping for clothes after work, but I didn't. "I was with another man," I answered painfully. "I'm sorry. Please believe me when I tell you it doesn't mean anything. It just happened."

Michael laughed bitterly. "I happen to think your having sex with another man means something," he replied, narrowing his eyes. "Are you in love with him?"

I shook my head. "No," I said truthfully. "He's just someone…."

"Who you cheated with," he finished for me. "You know, it would actually be easier I think if you did love him. Then maybe I could understand why you did it. I actually thought you were happy with me."

I started to cry then. "Michael, I'm really sorry," I sobbed. "I don't expect you to forgive me..."

"Yes, you do," he interrupted again. "You think I'm so head-over-heels in love with you, that I'll forgive anything you do. Well, sorry, it's not going to work this time. I'm not an idiot."

"We can work this out," I pleaded. "You can punish me somehow. I know I deserve it."

He shook his head. "I know I'm old enough to be your father," he answered coldly. "But I don't think of you as my daughter. I can't just turn you over my knee and spank you until you've learned your lesson. Or send you to your room for a time-out. This is our marriage we're talking about. I expect you to be an adult and take responsibility for your actions."

While I watched, Michael packed a bag full of clothes. "I'll let you know in a few days where you can reach me," he said, not really looking at me. "I need time alone to think."

I was devastated by the loss. Suddenly, our whole world had turned upside down. I had to comfort Jason, who thought it was his fault for hurting his ankle, and break the news to Asha. When they realized what I had done to make him leave, they were furious with me.

"How could you, Mom?" Asha asked. "Michael is the first guy who's ever cared about all of us! Everything was going so good! How could you sleep with someone else?"

How could I explain it, when I didn't fully understand it myself? "I made a mistake," I admitted. "I had something really good going and I blew it."

"Well, then, fix it," Asha replied, frowning. "Call Michael and tell him you're never going to do it again."

I sighed. If it were only that easy, I thought. If only Michael could have turned me over his knee and paddled my bare bottom until he felt better. Or think of some other type of punishment that would allow us to stay together. But that was childish thinking and I knew it. I had to fix this somehow, but it had to be as a woman!

I cried myself to sleep that night, and called in sick to work the next day. What was I going to do? Finally, out of desperation, I called my mother and told her what had happened. To my surprise, she came right over.

She gave me a hug when I opened the door. "Sarey, Sarey," she said, shaking her head. "You've really done it this time, haven't you?"

I burst into tears. "I know," I replied. "He'll never forgive me."

My mother bustled into the kitchen and made a pot of coffee. "Is that what you want?" she asked bluntly. "Do you really want Michael or this other man you were sleeping with?"

I opened my mouth to answer, then shut it again. "I don't want David," I replied finally. "I never loved him."

"And you don't love Michael either," she said matter-of-factly. "He's a good, solid man, but he's not very exciting."

I nodded. "Yes," I whispered. "That's exactly how I feel. That's why I cheated with David."

My mother poured two cups of coffee and sat down with me at the kitchen table. "Sarey, you've always had some pretty mixed-up ideas about love," she began gently. "When you got pregnant by Patrick and Eddie, I thought you'd learned your lesson about falling in love with good-looking, worthless men. When Michael came along, I was so grateful.

"But now you've gone and fallen for some sweet-talking loser again," she continued. "And you've hurt Michael deeply. All because you still don't know what love is. Sex is important to a relationship, but it's not everything. In fact, sometimes good sex can be the most distracting thing in the world."

"It's not the sex," I said, suddenly realizing that was true. "It's... it's the excitement of someone new and making love when we know we could get caught. It's scary, but fun."

"And it's got you nothing," she said. "You're alone again with two children to raise. The sad part is, you probably really do love Michael. You simply haven't grown up enough to realize what true love is."

"It doesn't matter," I said, starting to cry. "Michael doesn't want me anymore."

"Michael is hurt," she said. "And confused by everything that's happened. He doesn't know what he wants right now. But I guarantee you he hasn't fallen out of love with you that easily."

"So he might come back?" I said hopefully.

She shook her head. "You're going to have to fight for him," she answered. "You've hurt his pride. It's not going to be easy to get him back. But, before you even try, you have to make sure you want him. You can't just play with his life."

When my mother left, I felt more confused than ever. The real question was whether I really wanted Michael as a husband, or simply someone to take care of me and Asha and Jason?

I did a lot of thinking over the next few days. I had been selfish and immature and made a lot of poor decisions in the past. I liked Michael and respected him. Our sex life was fine and we had a lot in common. But was that enough to base a marriage on? Shouldn't I be madly, passionately in love with my husband?

When Michael called to tell me where he was staying, I felt my heart leap at the sound of his voice. "Michael," I said softly. "I've missed you."

"Don't," he replied. "I don't want to hear it."

"I know you're mad," I said quickly. "I don't expect you to forgive me, but just listen. I…I'd like us to see a marriage counselor."

I could hear the surprise in his voice. "A marriage counselor?" he repeated. "Why would you suggest that?"

"Look, I don't know how you feel about me," I replied. "But I've done nothing but think about our marriage for the last three days. I want us to be back together. I love you. I know that I do."

"I'm not interested in being a good provider anymore," he said bitterly. "Or a father figure. Or some kind of bumbling idiot who looks the other way while his wife has an affair."

"I know," I said simply. "I don't want that either. I never meant for you to feel like a fool."

"Sarey, maybe it would be better if we just split up," he said. "I'm not sure I want to give us a second chance."

"Please, Michael," I said, starting to cry.

"Okay," he agreed reluctantly. "I'll go with you to the marriage counselor. But I'm not promising anything."

I didn't even know how to find a marriage counselor, but I made about a dozen phone calls until I found Dr. Connors. "I need an appointment right away," I told her secretary. "It's an emergency."

She laughed. "They all are," she answered matter-of-factly. "But, fortunately, Dr. Connors had a cancellation. She can see you both tomorrow afternoon."

I called Michael about the appointment right away. "Can you make it?" I asked desperately.

"Yes," he grumbled. "But I don't see how it's going to help to tell all our problems to a perfect stranger."

Part of me felt exactly the same way, but I also wanted our marriage to work. "I'm sorry," I apologized for about the hundredth time. "I appreciate your going with me."

"I'll see you there," he replied briskly.

I didn't sleep much that night, and I must have changed outfits 10 times before going to Dr. Connors' office. When I saw Michael, I felt so nervous, I might faint. "Hi," I said softly.

"Hi, Sarey," he answered. It wasn't the most cordial of all greetings, but he had shown up.

For the first hour of our visit, Michael and I had to discuss our relationship, how we met and what our marriage was like. Finally, I revealed what had brought us to the doctor's office in the first place. It was embarrassing, and very painful, but I felt better talking about it.

Dr. Connors told us both to sit down facing each other. "Before we begin to fix this marriage," she said warmly. "The fact that you're both here is a good indication that there is hope for your marriage.

However, a strong relationship takes hard work. It takes compromise and caring about the other person – sometimes, more than you care about yourself. It's more than 50-50 give-and-take, it's 100-100."

"I gave all that," Michael protested, shooting me an angry look. "I didn't cheat on Sarey. She cheated on me."

"And we'll discuss that," Dr. Connors promised. "You feel angry and betrayed, Michael, but cheating on a spouse is often a sign of something else. Perhaps Sarey is trying to tell you something else."

"Like what?" he demanded, outraged.

"Like maybe Sarey felt pushed into marriage," Dr. Connors answered calmly. "You were older and more stable and she trusted you to know it was the right thing. In a way, Sarey has never had a chance to figure out what a real marriage is. She was a mother at a very young age."

Michael frowned. "So it's my fault she cheated on me with some young stud?" he asked in amazement.

Dr. Connors shook her head. "Of course not," she said kindly. "Sarey made that choice. She regrets it, obviously, but we need to make sure it doesn't happen again. The only way we can do that is to find out why she did it.

"Sarey," Dr. Connors continued. "Before our next appointment, I want you to write down a list of all your strengths and weaknesses. Perhaps the reason you are attracted to other men is because you feel that's your only worth."

"And what am I supposed to do?" Michael asked.

"I want you to sit down and write a list of reasons you believe that your and Sarey belong together," she replied. "And make sure they're good and solid. Love is a very powerful emotion, but it can do a great deal of damage as well as good. You don't always have to be the 'father figure' in this marriage. You're allowed to be the child once in a while."

"Dr. Connors," I began timidly. "Can we see each other during the week?"

"That's up to you," she replied easily. "This is your marriage."

When we went out into the waiting room, I turned to Michael. "Would you like to have dinner with me?" she asked.

He hesitated. "Okay," he replied. "But just dinner."

That hurt, but I tried not to let it show. We drove to a small Chinese restaurant near the doctor's office. When we were seated, there was a long awkward pause. Finally Michael spoke.

"You look nice, Sarey," he said at last.

"So do you, Michael," I answered. "I've missed you. The kids have missed you, too."

He nodded. "I feel pretty bad about that," he replied. "None of he said he would and we went straight to Joe's. Yolanda was already there and they were drinking some Hennessey when we walked in. This was the first time I had ever seen Joe. I'll say that he was every much as bit handsome as John was, but I tried not to look too hard.

We drank and laughed and talked about different things that didn't really matter in the world, but sure entertained us. I didn't care too much for Yolanda's arrogance, which she was full of, but I tolerated it for John.

Everyone drank liberally except for me. I only drank enough to get a little buzz. A buzz on me was probably like drunk on other people because I laughed a whole lot and I liked to get cuddly with my man.

Joe and Yolanda got to kissing pretty heavily and then made their way upstairs. It wasn't difficult to figure out what they were going to do. John and I were locked in a deep kiss of our own. I was running my hands over his soft, curly hair and he, with a gentle hand, caressed my face. Then that same gentle hand found it's way to one of my breasts. I gasped in delight for, although I was a virgin, I had let him hold my breasts in his hand before, like a sculptor and his clay masterpiece.

I loved the feeling it gave me when his hand would make it's way up my shirt and under my bra. It always sent a surge of energy through my body that would find its way to my sacred parts and make them tingle all within. His other hand found its way to my behind and rubbed and squeezed in that way that, when done together with the massaging my breasts, elicited soft sighs from me. This time he went further.

His hand went from my breast, lightly across my stomach, and to the button of my pants. They snapped open.

I hesitated, but only for a moment. I wanted him. I wanted him to satiate the tingling sensation between my thighs. I wanted to make love to him and I wanted him to make love to me. It was time.

I moved my hips in a way that would better help him do what he wanted to do and he reached his hand down my pants and began to massage my private area, but that only made me desire him more. "Oh, John. Take me now," I whispered into his ear. "Make love to me."

John helped me undress and this alone, being fully naked in front of a man for the first time, gave me added thrill. I wasn't worried about Joe or Yolanda coming downstairs. They would be busy themselves for awhile. When he was undressed, he laid me on my back and slid on top of me. He did nothing at first except to nuzzle my neck and nibble on my ears. Then he moved down my neck and across my chest and placed his mouth over one of my erect nipples, sucking on it and running his tongue across it. I reached down and began to manipulate this is their fault, but they're suffering because of our mistakes."

I felt even worse. "I know this whole thing is my fault," I said softly. "If there were any way I could take it back, I would."

Michael sighed. "No, it isn't, sweetheart," he said, shaking his head. "Look, I've been thinking about this ever since I found out about the other guy. I mean, I haven't been exactly honest with you either."

I felt my heart start to pound. "You had an affair?" I whispered in stunned disbelief.

He laughed. "No, but when I met and fell in love with you, I had my own selfish reasons for wanting us to be together," he replied. "I told you that Tina and I didn't have children. Well, the whole truth is that we tried for the last year of our marriage. We both went in to see a specialist. When I was tested, it turned out that I had a low sperm count. It would have been almost impossible for me to father a child.

"Tina and I weren't meant to be together," he continued calmly. "But that didn't help my feelings of inadequacy. When you came along, I fell in love with you – and your kids. It was a package deal. Deep down, I knew if I married you, I wouldn't have to answer questions about why I didn't have kids."

I was stunned. "You never said anything," I managed.

"You were so young and beautiful," he said, looking straight at me. "I knew I was too old for you, but that didn't stop me. It was selfish of me and I should have known better."

I had to smile. "So, somehow, the two of us found each other," I said. "Maybe we do belong together."

"I'd like to try to save our marriage," Michael answered. "I mean, if we do all the stuff the doctor wants us to, we should be okay. Maybe we can even come up with some ideas of our own."

I nodded. "I've already given notice at work," I said. "Michael, I can promise you I'll never cheat again. I mean it."

He nodded. "Let's go home and talk," he said tenderly.

Of course, it took a lot more work than that to put our marriage back together. We went for three months of counseling with Dr. Connors, and the most important thing we learned was that we needed to talk to each other about everything. The fact that we were married didn't mean we had stopped growing as people.

We didn't make love for a full month after we began counseling, even though Michael had already moved back home. That was Dr. Connors' suggestion as well. She said we needed to start fresh, and leave the past behind. But, when we finally did make love, it was incredible! I finally realized what it meant to be totally committed to another individual.

As for the future, I'm actually taking high school courses now and I hope to graduate so that I can enroll in college classes soon. I'm not trying to recapture my youth – I'm just looking forward to my future.

I know I'm lucky that Michael stood by me. Sometimes, if you're very lucky, life gives you a second chance.

THE END

CHEATING LOVERS
We Caught Our Spouses In The Act!

I remember the day I met John. We met in senior year of high school. I immediately fell in love with him. With his beautiful brown eyes and masculine body, not to mention his charming personality, how could I not?

I also remember when we divorced, but I'd get to that later.

John was on the varsity football team. He was one of the star players and high scorers of the team. He never made captain, but he was an inspiration to his team.

Yolanda was one of the cheerleaders for the team. She dated John's slightly older brother Joe, who had graduated the previous year. He too, was on the football team at one time, but was more into the intellectual pursuits. Yolanda and Joe would end up getting married, too.

I was still a virgin until we were near the end of our senior year. I also remember that night, but who doesn't when they lose their virginity.

I was at home doing what I did every weeknight; homework. The phone rang and I answered it. "Hello?"

"Hey, Tamika," John sang. "What are you doing tonight?"

"Trying to graduate," I answered.

"Let's go out tonight, baby. We can take Joe and Yolanda and hit the strip."

"I don't know" I was uncertain. I didn't want to be out all night and still have to get up early in the morning.

"Come on, baby doll," he was pleading now. "There's a party over at Smoke's. Everyone's going to be there!"

I said, "You know I don't like Smoke. Trouble always comes to his parties."

"No, Tamika. Everything will be straight. If anything goes down, we'll just leave."

I was too skeptical. "Like last time, right." Last time he ended up getting into a fight because someone had spilled a drink on him accidentally.

"Okay. You're right. We could all go to Joe's then. Have some drinks and a good time."

I thought about it a minute and said, "As long as we're back by eleven."

"Eleven it is. I'll be by in about half an hour." He came by when his throbbing manhood.

Then he lowered himself to me and slowly and gently he entered me. It hurt at first, but soon the waves of ecstasy washed over me. Our hot and sweat-soaked bodies moved in a synchronous rhythm, both of us moaning and kissing, whispering words of love into each other's ears.

I could have never imagined that sex could feel so wonderfully beautiful. The raw emotions pouring from the both of us, one working off the other's love. And then he began to climax. His body jerking in ecstatic spasms, his manhood throbbing even more inside me, and the warmth I felt explode within me caused my body to quake in a climax of my own, and our voices no doubt could be heard by Joe and Yolanda but I didn't care. I was in heaven and I didn't want to leave.

After, we laid there awhile, on the couch, holding each other and enjoying each other's warmth and love. We put our clothes back on and talked for a bit until Joe and Yolanda came back downstairs. I wasn't sure if I was being self-conscious or what, but I swear that they kept smiling at me as if to say, we know what you guys were doing. Maybe it was because of the smile that refused to leave my face or maybe we really were loud enough to hear upstairs. I've never regretted the experience, not even to this day.

We continuously repeated that night's events many times afterwards and every time was as good as the last.

We eventually graduated and Joe and Yolanda went down to Las Vegas for a week and got married. John and I waited for a more traditional wedding and spent many romantic and pleasurable nights waiting for it.

When we did get married, it was the most beautiful spectacle I had ever seen in my life and my mother and I couldn't stop crying. However, this gem of a wedding had one flaw in it; Yolanda was my bridesmaid. I only did it because she was married to John's brother and he was the best man. But regardless of her, we lived happily ever after-until about two months ago, because of her.

Naturally, responsibility set in and John had to get a job in a factory. We had both gotten cars for our graduation so we only had to pay for our house. The factory job, although it kept the bills paid, gradually began to eat up John's time. He got put on a lot of overtime and we spent some weeks with only a parting kiss to hold me over.

It got so tight for me at times that I tried self-stimulation, but that didn't do anything for me, so I made sure that when there was time for some loving between John and me, I made sure it was all the way good.

But as my mind wandered back, I reflected. I was at home one day in the evening when the phone rang. It was John.

"Hey, baby," he said. He still called me that. "I've got to do this overtime thing again."

I was disappointed. "Damn, John. Why do they always want you to do it?"

"How do you think I'm going to be a supervisor or foreman or something? I've got to show responsibility and all that."

"Yeah. I guess so. When are you going to be home?"

He thought for a minute and then said, "Around two in the morning."

I let out a surrendering sigh. "All right then," I said. "I'll leave some supper in the fridge for you, okay?"

He said, "That'll be fine, baby doll. I'll try not to wake you."

"You know, I don't have a problem with you waking me up-as long as you take care of this problem I'm having."

"What's that?" he asked.

"You know that tingling sensation I told you about?"

"Aw, baby. I can't. I'm going to be tired as all hell. I'm sorry baby."

"Yeah, it's alright, I guess." No. It wasn't alright, but he had a job to do. "Maybe tomorrow, then. You can say no if they ask you to work overtime."

He said, "It's a date, then. I got to go now, so I'll see you later, okay? I love you."

"I love you, too." And we hung up. I was mad. Mad because he wouldn't tell his boss he was sick or something. Well, he was trying to make ends meet. I could forgive him for that. So, while I was home alone, I figured I might as well go out and rent a movie.

I got into my car and took the long way to the video rental. I was thinking maybe getting a romance or a comedy or maybe through the selections. I ran into Joe.

"Hey, Tamika," he said.

"Hey! What's up?" I asked.

"Nothing really. Yolanda had to go and baby-sit her niece. I'm just here to get a movie to watch."

"Yeah, John's doing some overtime so I'm getting one too. What are you looking for?"

He thought a moment and said, "I'm thinking romantic comedy or something."

"I was thinking the same thing. We must be psychic," I laughed.

"You know," he said. "We should all get together some time. We rarely see each other anymore with John working all the time."

"That sounds like a good idea. I'll ask John and see what he thinks." We talked a little while longer and then said our good-byes. I found a suitable movie then took the long way home. On the way,

I had to stop at a red light. There I saw something I didn't like at all.

Not too far up the street is one of those cheap motels. It was called the Overnight Motel. The sign even said it had cable. The parking lot didn't have many cars in it tonight, but there was one car in particular that I saw. It was John's.

John's car was in the parking lot of the seedy motel. John was supposed to be at work, therefore his car should have been there at his job. I looked around the building and there was none other than John himself, walking up the steps to a room. That in itself was bad, but what was worse than that was the fact that he was holding the hand of his brother's wife, Yolanda. I just stared at the whole scene.

A car horn jolted me from my gawking at the motel and then I noticed the light was now green. I drove on, staring straight ahead of me, my hands trembling, my mind racing at a million miles an hour. I was too scared to go and confront them. I wasn't ready for that, but I needed someone to talk to. Who better than the woman's husband who my husband was cheating with. So, I drove to Joe's.

I dreaded telling him the news, but I had to for both of our sakes. My hands were still trembling when I got there. I rang the doorbell. It seemed like it took him forever to answer the door and I almost lost the nerve I had built up, but he answered it before I could run.

"Hey, Tamika, what's wrong? Come in." He opened the door and I stepped in. I went to the couch and sat, but said nothing.

"Tamika," he said, sitting next to me. "What is it? Oh God, please don't tell me something has happened to John..." His tone had gotten quieter, fearing what I might have had to say.

I said, "John-John," then the tears began to swell. I blurted out, "John and Yolanda are at a motel together."

He stood up. "What?" he asked incredulously. "What kind of joke is that?"

"They're there right now. I'm telling you the truth."

"You wait here. I'll be back. Where are they?" he asked. I told him and he walked out the front door, got into his car, and drove off.

I waited and waited for what seemed to be an eternity. My mind was a jumble of mixed emotions and the more I thought about it, the more angrier I got. What about all the other times he had to work late? Was he out with her? Were there others? Had he been doing this for a long time? Why was he doing it all alone?

He would pay, I thought.

Joe finally came back. When he came in, he had tears in his eyes. "I can't believe it," he said. "He's my own brother. We're blood."

"Joe," I said, standing up and putting my arm around him. "They're nothing. Now we know their true colors. They've been lying to us-" He cut me off.

"What do you mean 'been lying'? As far as we know, this is the only time this has happened."

"Well, John's been getting an awful lot of overtime ever since he got that stupid job. And add to the fact that my sex life at home has been dull as of late. You know, as if he were already getting his rocks off somewhere else."

Joe appeared to be mulling that over in his mind and then said with the look of realization in his eyes, "You know, she's been doing these odd jobs a lot. They always require her to stay out real late, but says the money is in a bank account she set aside."

I was shocked although I shouldn't have been. I said, "John's been telling me that same line, too."

"Then what do we do about this, Tamika?"

I thought on this next part. Would what I do next be just as wrong? I didn't care. Not anymore. I stepped from his side to in front of him and I kissed him. He put up resistance. "Tamika, what the hell-" I cut him off with my lips. He slowly started to give in. I put my arms around him and, hesitating only a moment, he put his arms around me. That's where I began to get nervous. Not because of what we were doing, but I had never been with anyone other than John. This was exciting.

His hands slowly moved from the small of my back down to my buttocks and he was rubbing and squeezing me. He stopped kissing me only to run his lips and his tongue across my neck. I moaned a sigh of encouragement. "Let's go to the bedroom, Joe," I suggested.

I began to realize just how much like John he was. Soft, gentle hands, a wonderful kiss. He was also handsome and well-built. I wanted to find out whether or not he was as well-endowed.

He took my hand in his and led me into his bedroom where, fittingly, he shared Yolanda.

He took me in both hands and lowered me onto the bed. He took my feet in his hands and took my shoes and socks off. Joe began to caress them with his lips, sending shivers all throughout my body, making my special place go all tingly. He then moved on top of me and kissed a passionate kiss and said, "You don't know it, but I've always wanted you. You're so beautiful, smart and sexy."

And he started unbuttoning my shirt until my bra was showing. The bra's latch was in the front, so that made it easy for him to unsnap it. I felt his breath on my exposed breasts before his tongue made contact with my erect nipple. His hand was busy exploring my other breast as I rubbed my hands on his muscled back.

He lifted off me and, staring into my eyes, he unbuttoned and unzipped my pants and slowly yet steadily he pulled them down, first over my hips, then down my legs until they were off. He repeated his actions with my panties. He then undressed himself while I watched. He wasn't showing off or anything like that, but I wanted him more than I ever had at that moment.

"Come to me," I whispered, holding my arms out to him. He obeyed and fell into my arms and we kissed a deep kiss that lasted for an eternity. I realized then that what I felt for him was love. He was everything John was and more. "I love you ," I whispered in his ear.

"Oh God, Tamika. I love you, too," he said so passionately.

I rolled him over on his back and climbed onto his manhood and I felt instantaneous pleasure as he entered me.

Palms on his chiseled chest, I began to move up and down, slowly at first until he began to move with me and we picked up speed.

The intensity between us built higher and higher as our rhythmic bodies moved faster and faster. Our breathing got steadily heavier and the sweat was dripping from off our heated bodies. I felt his movements become jerky and he squeezed my buttocks tight. His thrusts were harder and harder, deeper and deeper. I cried out in pleasure as he climaxed inside of me while I reached mine at the same time. Our bodies convulsed and writhed in throes of our passion.

"Joe. Oh yes, Joe!" I cried out, as the finale of thrusts were ending. He slowed his movements until he came to a complete stop.

"Tamika," he said, out of breath. "You don't know how long I've wanted you. So close to you, yet so far at the same time. I love you, Tamika."

"Joe," I couldn't think of what to say. "Oh, Joe, I love you, too."

"So what now?" he asked.

Cuddling up beside him, lacing my fingers along his chest, I said, "We could run and away together and start our lives over. Or we could divorce our unfaithful spouses and we could marry."

"Yeah. I like the sound of the last one. How do we tell them about it?"

Smiling, I said, "We wait. We wait until they do it again and then we bust them in the act."

Joe frowned. "I don't know if I could live with her until she does it again. What if they take forever, or if this was a one time thing?"

My tracing finger made a line down his stomach until it reached between his legs and I stroked him once again. The response was almost immediate. Then I said, "We can console each other until then."

"I like the sound of that," he commented, and we made sweet love one more time that night.

The next few days after I discovered John and Yolanda having extramarital relations with each other were some of the worst days of my life. I pretended not to know anything that he did that night. I even went so far as to have sex with him. I had never turned him down before and I didn't want to arouse his suspicion.

Joe and I had not seen each other again since that night we shared each other's love, but I thought of him everyday. I thought about the night we spent in each other's arms and fantasized about the future nights to come. His breathtaking kiss, hard body, and the way he made me feel. Our day would come.

John had kept his promise to take the day off and spend it with me, although that was too little, too late. Otherwise, things weren't much different and it inflamed me that he could so unscrupulously sleep with his brother's wife, not to mention cheat on his own wife, me, without any guilt whatsoever! I, myself, felt no guilt for sleeping with Joe, but not because I felt justified in the 'you did it to me, now I'm doing it to you' kind of way, although that was the initial reason for it. I might not have always loved him, but it grew over the years of knowing him and being around him.

As I said, the next few days were some of the worst in my life as I was disgusted with my husband, disgusted at his callosity. However, he predictably called me from work to say that he would be coming in late. About twenty minutes after he hung up, I called Joe. He answered the phone.

"Hello?"

I wasted no time. "He's working late tonight. Is Yolanda there?"

"Hey, Tamika," he said. "No. She just happened to go baby-sitting her niece again."

I was nodding even though he couldn't see me. "Good. I'll be by in about ten minutes." I paused then said, "I love you."

"I love you too, Tamika," and we hung up.

When I got into my car, I realized that I was not angry at John. I was more elated because this would be the night that Joe and I could openly admit our feelings toward each other. Later we could marry, but not until after we got to know each other well enough. John had raised that safeguard in me.

I purposely avoided driving down any road that John or Yolanda might be on for fear that my car would be recognized. When I got there, Joe was waiting on the porch. He came to the car and got in. "Where do we start first," he asked.

"The same place I caught them the first time."

"Sounds like a plan."

We drove to the Overnight Motel, but there was no car I recognized. We then drove around the city for quite some time checking out motel after motel without any luck. We started looking into back alleys and on back roads and still there was no sign of the two anywhere.

We hadn't said much the entire time we were looking for them, but I could tell he was anxious. Anxious to get this over with or anxious because he just might actually find his wife with my husband in bed together. I wanted to comfort him, but we had a job to do that night. There would be plenty of time for comfort later.

So we checked the motels again and back-tracked other areas we had been through. Still there was no sign of them. "What are we going to do now?" I asked.

"I don't know. They've got themselves a good hiding spot this time. Or maybe it was a one time thing."

What he said struck a chord with me. What if it really was a one time thing? A lapse in judgment? Even if it was a one time thing, could I still forgive him?

"We can stop by her sister's house," Joe suggested. "If Yolanda's there then I guess they're not doing it anymore."

I didn't like the implications of that. I said, "And if she's there and not screwing my husband what does that mean for us?"

He was quiet for a moment before saying, "We'll just have to work it out."

That's exactly what we would have to do then. I knew I loved Joe and that John cheated on me. That was enough for me. But for Joe, he would have to answer his own life's questions. After all, from his way of thinking, he didn't actually see my husband and his wife making love together and he would be, and has, made love to his brother's wife. And what if, by some miraculous chance, we were wrong about them?

I had no doubts about their infidelity, but I knew that, until we caught them in the act or they confessed, he would have such doubts.

"Then let's go," I said, and we rode off to Yolanda's sister's house.

When we got there, my heart sank. Was I wrong? Was I the one who was cheating? There in the driveway was Yolanda's car. My husband's was no where around. Joe just looked at me with what may have been regret. We got out of the car and headed towards the door of the house. None of the lights were on. He rang the doorbell. No answer. He waited and then rang it again. Still, no answer. "Maybe she's sleeping," he said. I wasn't ready to give up.

No lights, no answer. I thought she was out with John somewhere. That could be why his car wasn't here. I told him as much.

"No," he said in answer. "Let's check some windows. Maybe she's sleeping like I said."

So we went around the house looking window to window. First the living room, then the kitchen, then what bedrooms were on ground level. Nothing of worth to note. On our way back to the car, I saw a small window leading into a basement room. I pointed it out to Joe. We both looked in.

In the window we saw Yolanda lying on a blanket on the floor. Naked with John on top of her, the two of them in the act. Joe was speechless, his mouth hanging open and his eyes wide. "That no good little-" He let the rest of the sentence trail off.

I grabbed his hand and whispered, "Don't sweat it. Now it's out in the open and we can be together." I smiled when I said it, but I can't say that I didn't feel hurt myself. We had taken vows. I had given myself to him. I had loved John. But that was done with. My heart belonged to another now.

Joe knocked on the window as we stared in on them. John jumped as if a rat had ran across his leg. When he saw us, I would have to say that the look on his face was worth all of the feelings of betrayal he caused. Yolanda, too, was shocked back into the real world. She looked ready to cry when she saw who it was in the window. We got up and walked to the front of the house. There we waited for the duplicitous duo. The door opened. It was John.

When he came out, he was fully dressed and looked timid. "Look," he said. "It's not what it seems."

Joe stepped forward and said, "You mother-" I cut him off before something happened that we would all regret.

I said, "Oh, so what is it? Wrestling? Innocent massage? Please tell me because I'd sure like to hear it."

John said, "Please, baby. I don't know what came over me. She came on to me and I fell into it. I've never done anything like this before. I swear."

"That is, before three nights ago at that motel, right," asked Joe. John was speechless. "You, my brother, sleeping with my wife. How dare you?"

"But-"

I cut John off. "What comes around goes around. I hope you two are happy together because I know Joe and I will be."

He was taken aback. "What?"

Joe said, "Yeah. So you can tell Yolanda that her stuff will be here tomorrow. I don't even want to see her face."

Joe and I turned to leave. As we were making our way to the car, John kept calling my name and saying he was sorry. I ignored him easily.

We headed back to Joe's house and he was quiet all the way. When we got there I asked, "Are you going to be alright?"

He gave me a half smile and said, "Yeah, I guess so. Do you want to come in?"

I liked the sound of that. "Yeah."

We stepped into the house and he turned the lights on. "Would you like something to drink," he asked.

I told him I would and he brought back two glasses of red wine. He sat down next to me and handed me a glass. "To the future," he said.

I repeated his sentiments. "To the future." We tipped glasses and drank. I was happy with him and knew that I would always be happy with him. He leaned forward and kissed me, his hand on my hip. I was unbuttoning his shirt, running my hands across his masculine chest. His caressing lips found their way to my soft neck, sending shivers throughout my body. I could stand no more.

I took my shirt off and unhooked my bra and guided his mouth to my nipple. How I loved that. He massaged and manipulated my breasts, knowing just how to make my body tingle.

He then took my hand and made an attempt to take me to his bedroom, but we never made it.

We stopped along the way, kissing in frenzied passion. He backed me against the wall and, as our bodies pressed together. I felt the stiffness in his pants against the wetness of mine. "Oh, take me Joe," I whispered in his ear. "Right here, right now."

We all but tore each other's clothes off, touching and feeling along the way. He lifted me off my feet and I wrapped my legs around him, his hands on my bottom, holding me up. Slowly, I felt his love enter me. He pushed in and pulled out, pushed in, pulled out, each thrust taking me to new levels of ecstasy I had never felt before. I called out his name repeatedly, begging him for more. He gave me all that I asked for plus some. He gave two extraordinary thrusts and he began his climax, filling me with his warm love. I began my orgasmic climax and cried out in pleasure at the finish.

That night we laid together many more times and laid together many nights after that, but they never seemed to last long enough. Joe and I lived together now, so that was no longer a problem.

John had gotten his things and Yolanda's too. I guess she was too ashamed to face Joe. I would hear from John in the future, but for all his pleading, I didn't care.

The past was far behind us.

THE END

SEX ON THE SIDE
I Was Carrying Another Man's Baby

I was crying again. Tyrone and I had just had another fight. It seemed that was all we did lately, and always about the same thing, Tyrone's obsession with his job. He designed programs for computers. He had worked hard to get this job and he loved it. Sometimes I think he loved his work more than he loved me. When a new job came into his company, Tyrone was the one to travel to the new client to access his needs. He never hesitated, telling me that it was all for our future.

"Jo, Baby. Soon we'll be able to build that house we always dreamed of, and then we can start raising a family."

The house was his dream, not mine. I just wanted to buy a little house that we could afford and settle down to raise a family. Instead I had taken a job as a waitress to pass the time because Tyrone was out of town so often. Now I got up from our bed and went to take a shower. Tyrone was gone again and I had a job to go to. I worked the evening shift and it was time to get ready.

Later at the restaurant, I tried to forget the angry words Tyrone and I had exchanged before he packed his bag and walked out the door. I stood looking out the window at the mist-shrouded mountains across the field. They were so close that I could see the pine trees as they disappeared into the clouds. The view was the only good thing about this place. We were out in the middle of nowhere but only a few minutes from Exit 12 of the Interstate Highway. Our customers were mostly travelers and truckers. An icy early spring rain was falling and the only spot of color I saw was the red cab of a sixteen wheeler as it maneuvered into a parking space.

The driver climbed down and hurried into the shelter of the restaurant. I moved away from the window and tied the white apron over my pink waitress uniform. I had shortened the hem and taken in the waist to spite Tyrone. The uniform fit like wallpaper. Ed, the owner, complained to me about it at least once a week.

"Josephine that uniform is too short. You should let the hem down about two inches."

I ignored him. We both knew good help was hard to find in this out of the way place and Ed would not risk losing a good waitress.

My eyes returned to the trucker as he slid into the corner booth, his well-shaped thighs filled out the tight jeans he wore. He took off his cap and laid it on the seat beside him. A few dark curls fell over his prominent widow's peak. It gave him a devilish look. As I approached his booth, I saw the usual look of appreciation light up his dark eyes at the way my uniform stretched tight across my breasts. Tantalizing the truckers was the only amusement I had in this dull place and I held the order pad in front of me as I spoke in my most seductive voice.

"What would you like, Sir."

His lazy smile showed even white teeth in his dark face.

"A good looking girl like you should never ask a tired truck driver what he would like," he teased.

"You're right. This is a truck stop after all. But it's a slow night." I watched his eyes slide to the buttons straining across my breasts and I could tell his mind slid from steak to sex in a mini second. I stood patiently as his gaze traveled over the rest of my body and returned to my face. At least someone appreciates me, I thought.

"Your order sir?"

"Oh," he stammered, bringing his mind back to the present "A steak, French fries and strong coffee. I think I want to stay awake for awhile."

"Yes, sir." I turned and walked into the kitchen and gave his order to the cook. I refilled the coffee cups of an old couple, the only other people in the restaurant, then carried the coffeepot to the trucker and filled his mug.

"Would you like sweetener, Sir," I drawled.

"That depends on whose supplying the sugar," he came right back at me.

"M-m-m, we'll see," I answered as I sauntered back to the kitchen. The old couple paid their bill and left.

When I carried the steaming steak and French fries over to the corner booth, the trucker said.

"Since it's such a slow night, can you sit awhile?" I slid into the booth opposite him.

"My name's Bernie. What's yours?"

"They call me Jo, short for Josephine."

"The weather's getting pretty bad out there," he said.

"It happens this time of year. Spring is so unpredictable. All those little things in the ground growing. It makes my blood run hot," I said, lifting the hair from the back of my neck.

The fork stopped halfway to his mouth. "What time do you get off work?" he asked.

A warning red light flashed in the back of my mind but I ignored it.

"Where are you headed?" I asked.

"New Jersey to deliver a house full of furniture. Lots of people move to New Jersey. I should be back here again in three days, but I'm staying here tonight."

I rose as new people came through the door. "I gotta take care of these customers."

"Hurry back," he called after me.

Each time I looked up Bernie's eyes were on me and I felt a fire beginning in my loins and there was no one at home to quench it.

At about twelve thirty, I brought two beers and sat down across from him. He was the most exciting man I had seen all week. It can be pretty dull around here. The fire was now raging inside me and I was not about to let it go out.

"So Bernie, What room are you in?"

He reached for the key in his pocket. "One ten. Is it far?"

I reached for his hand. "Come on, I'll show you a short cut."

He grabbed his bag and followed me through the kitchen.

We entered his room and closed the door. I turned to him and unbuttoned his shirt. The suspense had been building all evening and now I was ready for action. I slipped out of my uniform as he removed his clothes and in a few minutes we stood naked in front of each other.

I turned around slowly. "You like what you see?" I asked.

"Girl, you don't need to ask that question," he said, pulling me to the bed.

"I can see that," I replied, reaching for his erect manhood. His palms were rough as they moved lightly over my body. I used my tongue slowly around the tattoo on his shoulder. He shuddered as my fingers moved up and down slowly and then faster. The smoldering flame inside me burst into fire as he pulled me on top of him and entered me quickly. I matched his rhythm and in a few moments we reached a climax. He let out a long sigh and we fell asleep in each other's arms.

When I woke a little bit later, Bernie was looking at me in the blinking blue light that shown through the window. "Don't you have to go home?" he asked.

"It's cold out there," I said drowsily. "Mind if I stay here?" I snuggled up to him and before long we were both asleep again.

When I awoke the next morning, Bernie had showered and shaved and he stood before me clad only in his shorts. He looked very powerful, his bronze shoulders broad and muscular. He came over to the bed.

"M-m-m," I said and pulled him down beside me. I slid down his shorts and ran my fingers along the strong muscles in his back and buttocks and brought my hands around to the front of his body. His callused fingers stroked my nipples into tight buds.

He rose up on his elbows. "Oh, Baby, I wish I could take you with me. There's plenty of room in my truck. You ever made love in a sixteen wheeler?" he chuckled. I pulled him to me, bare chest to bare chest.

"Shut up and kiss me," I said. Instead he entered me roughly and brought me to fulfillment before taking his own release. When we again lay spent, I asked.

"How long is it going to be before you come back this way?"

"Three days. That is if I get started today." He reached for me again.

"Well then, you'd better get rolling," I said jumping out of bed and heading for the bathroom. "Hurry back. I'll be waiting," I chimed as I closed the door.

When I came out of the bathroom the room was empty. I slipped into my uniform and headed for the restaurant for some breakfast.

By the time I had finished, the ice on the roads was starting to melt and I drove home. When I walked into the empty rooms my guilty conscience reared its head.

While changing my clothes I thought of Tyrone. I began to clean the kitchen, then the bathroom. By the time I had finished, the rooms were shining. I went to work that night but decided I would call off sick the next day. Bernie was due back and I could not meet him again.

The next day when I saw my handsome husband walk through the door, I was so ashamed I blushed under my dark skin. Tyrone kissed me and then looked closely at my face.

"What's the matter Honey? Don't you feel well?"

"As a matter of fact I called in sick. I want to stay home with my husband tonight."

"Sounds good, Baby. We have some things to talk about."

My heart sank. Did he know about Bernie? He couldn't possibly have found out.

I had roasted a small chicken and we sat down to a meal complete with baked potatoes and salad. After dinner Tyrone took my hand.

"Come into the living room," he said.

"I'd better clean up first," I held back.

"Let the dishes sit. I'll help you later."

I could feel the sweat dropping between my breasts as he pulled me down beside him on the couch. "Honey, we're almost there."

"Where?" I croaked.

"We almost have enough money in the bank for the down payment on my dream house. When I get my next pay you can quit your job and we'll be able to start looking at lots."

"Where do you want to look?" I asked.

"I thought we would start in Hamilton Hills."

"Hamilton Hills, that's a pretty expensive development."

"We can afford it, Baby. I got a promotion last week and it means that I won't have to travel so much."

"Oh, Tyrone, that's wonderful." I threw my arms around his neck.

As we were cleaning up the dishes Tyrone talked constantly about the lot he would buy and the house he would design.

"It will have double front doors and a separate room just for the computer."

"And a nursery," I added taking his hand. "Let's go make a baby to put in that nursery."

I pulled down the spread on our queen-sized bed, slipped out of my clothes and lay down. "Come to mama," I said stretching my arms wide.

Tyrone quickly shed his clothes and lay down beside me. He began caressing my body with his smooth hands. I quickly dismissed the thought of those rough hands that brought me such ecstasy two days ago. I ran my fingers over the fine dark hair on his chest. I closed my eyes so I could feel the touch of his lips on my breast, his fiery tongue, teasing my nipples into hard peaks. The old familiar shiver rippled through me. He stretched out fully now and I could feel his swollen shaft against my thigh. The caress of his lips on my mouth and along my body set me aflame. Tyrone was on top of me.

"Shall we make a girl or a boy?" he teased. He started with slow, deep, full thrusts, then alternated with short hard thrusts. I rose to meet his rhythm and together we reached a climax that set the stars bursting in my head. We lay for awhile with Tyrone's arms around me and then I pulled up the covers and we fell asleep.

Later that week I went back to work but I switched to the afternoon schedule so I could be home in the evenings when Tyrone was home. We went to look at lots in the Hamilton Hills plan which was closer to my parents. I was their only child and they had been throwing hints for months about Tyrone and I having children.

"When are you going to give Dad and me a grandchild?" Mom asked about once a week. I knew they would be pleased to have us living closer to them.

My husband began bringing home pictures of houses that would fit in that plan. I couldn't believe some of the houses.

"Honey, are you sure we can afford a house this grand?" I asked him.

"Sweetheart, don't worry about the money. I just want you to enjoy this house."

On a Sunday evening in June we took some of the plans over to my Mom and Dad. Mom could hardly contain her excitement. She hugged me.

"Oh, Jo, your father and I have wanted a grandchild for such a long time. Are you two or three months along?"

I looked at Mom. "What do you mean?" I asked.

"You're pregnant, aren't you?"

I looked at Tyrone. I had been gaining a little weight lately but with all the excitement about our new house I didn't pay much attention to it. Then I began to think back two months, three months. I couldn't remember when my last period was.

I looked down at my expanding waistline and then Tyrone was beside me.

"Well, we've certainly been trying hard enough lately," he said laying his hand on my stomach. I think we'll be paying a visit to the doctor next week."

Mom brought out the cake she had baked that afternoon and we sat around the table looking at blueprints for houses. When we were ready to leave, Mom gave me a big hug and whispered, "Let me know as soon as you come from the doctor."

I rode home beside Tyrone, my mind in a daze. I thought back over the two months and three months. I was glad Tyrone could not read my mind there in the dark. It must have been that time we made love after Tyrone told me that we would be able to buy a house. But just two days before that I had been with another man. Silently I prayed that the baby would look like me or my husband.

On Wednesday Tyrone took the afternoon off and went with me to see the doctor. He sat in the waiting room while Dr. Taylor informed me that I was indeed about three months pregnant. He prescribed prenatal vitamins and told me to make an appointment with Dr. Hartmen, the gynecologist.

Tyrone was overjoyed. He hoped it would be a boy but if not we would try again and have a boy the second time. Tyrone was very solicitous telling me to not work too hard around the house and get plenty of exercise and eat a lot of fruit and vegetables.

The next week we picked out a lot on a dead end street in Hamilton Hills. Tyrone made an appointment with a contractor and was having the best time of his life planning our house. The nursery would be next to our bedroom and the extra bedrooms down the hall with their own bath at that end of the house. The double entry doors would open up into an impressive hallway with a grand stairway leading to the second floor. There would be a large bright kitchen looking out on the back yard where I could watch our children play.

"Tyrone, we don't have enough furniture to fill up a house this big," I told him.

"Don't worry, Baby. We'll buy all the furniture we need."

I began to wonder if Tyrone had robbed a bank sometime in the past. He seemed to have plenty of money. Mom and Dad drove over to look at the lot and Dad wanted to know when construction would begin. My mom went with me to the mall to buy maternity clothes. I had quit my job as soon as my uniform got too tight to wear.

"Josephine, I hope you realize how lucky you are," Mom said. "married to a man like Tyrone and building a new house. Now you know why he worked so hard for five years."

"Yes, Mom," I said to myself. If only I had realized it six months ago.

Construction was scheduled to begin just after Christmas but Tyrone decided to put it off until after the baby was born. The distraction of the holidays was over and the days seemed to drag by endlessly. The doctor had told me to expect the baby any time and I sat around the apartment watching TV and waiting. On January fifth, the pains began low in my back. Tyrone refused to go to work. My bag was packed and he moved it to the front door. He kept urging me to go to the hospital.

"Don't fuss, Tyrone," I told him. "The doctor said to wait until the pains are five minutes apart." I started to time them and realized they were five minutes apart and getting stronger all the time.

"Well, grab the bag and let's go!" I continued.

Tyrone just stood there for a minute before he picked up the bag and hurried down the hall, leaving me to put on my coat and follow him.

At the hospital the doctor examined me and said since this was my first child that I might be in labor for hours. He told Tyrone to go have a cup of coffee. My husband left and went to call my parents. By the time he returned the doctor told him to scrub up. We were going to the delivery room. I don't remember much after that until a lusty cry broke through the fog in my brain and Tyrone was leaning over me saying, "Jo, wake up. Our son is calling you."

The nurse brought him then, wrapped in a blue blanket, his tiny fist curled in a ball and trying to find its way to his mouth. If our child was a boy we had decided to name him Robert after Tyrone's father who had passed away two years ago. Tyrone was so excited.

"He knows me, Jo. He looked right at me." I smiled at my proud husband and looked at our baby boy. A miniature human being with lots of dark hair plastered to his head.

"I'll take him now and clean him up," the nurse said. "You need to sleep."

Tyrone kissed me on the forehead. "Sleep now Sweetheart, I'll be back later." I fell asleep thinking it was the happiest moment I could ever remember.

My happiness changed to fear later that day when little Robbie was brought to me again. He had been cleaned up and his hair brushed away from his forehead. A deep widow's peak was clearly visible with a curl falling down over his forehead. My tears began to fall on the blue blanket. This was not Tyrone's baby. There was no mistaking the widows peak that matched Bernie's and was so different from either Tyrone's or my family. Just then my husband walked in.

"Isn't he beautiful?" he asked. Then noticing my tears, he said tenderly. "Don't cry Sweetheart. The worst is over."

Oh God, I prayed, please let him be right.

When Mom and Dad came to see me that evening I was bathed and feeding little Robbie his first bottle. Mom was the one who remarked on Robbie's hairline.

"Isn't that strange," she said. "None of our relatives have hair like that."

"Oh, Mom," I said. "His hair will probably change as he gets older. I'm just glad he's healthy."

"You're right sweetheart," she said as she ran her hand gently over his small head.

The next months were the happiest time of our marriage. Little Robbie thrived. Tyrone was busy working with the contractor on our new house. The only cloud on my horizon was the prayer I said each evening as I lay down to sleep.

"Dear Lord, please don't ever let Tyrone and Bernie meet each other."

After awhile my fear faded. Things were going so well. Tyrone was home most nights except when he was meeting with the contractor. The workmen had started construction on our new house and each evening we rode over to see the progress. Next week the bricks would be in place. We should have been able to move in by the time Robbie was a year old.

At ten months, our son was already walking, keeping me busy chasing him everywhere. I tried to brush his hair forward so the widow's peak was not so noticeable but the stubborn curl fell forward on his forehead. Back in our apartment there were boxes sitting everywhere. Everything that we were not using was packed in boxes waiting for the movers. I had told Tyrone I would arrange for the moving company. I wanted to be sure he did not call the WorldWide Moving Company even though I knew Bernie worked out of Pittsburgh.

I had arranged a birthday party for Robbie's first birthday. We had balloons and a big chocolate cake decorated with a clown. Mom and Dad came over and for once Robbie was allowed to stuff his mouth with cake. We all laughed and took lots of pictures. I tried not to think of the muscular man with the curls on his forehead that Robbie resembled.

The next day Tyrone and I took Robbie over to our new house. It was almost finished and I wanted to arrange for a moving company the middle of next month. As we got closer to the house we saw a big moving van parked next door. Our neighbors were moving in to their new house. A lump rose in my throat and I felt like I could not breathe when I saw the big red letters on the truck. 'Worldwide Movers'.

As soon as Tyrone stopped the car I unbuckled Robbie's seat belt and hurried inside our house. I tried to keep Robbie away from the windows but he loved the wide-open spaces of an empty house and I had to chase after him to keep him from falling down. I didn't notice that Tyrone had gone over to the driver of the big truck and asked him to give us a bid on moving our furniture into the new house.

When he came back and told me what he had done I screamed at him. "My God, why did you do that? I told you I would take care of it."

Tyrone looked at me like I had slapped him in the face. "Jo, why are you getting so excited? What can it hurt for us to have more than one bid? We'll use whoever gives us the best price."

I hung my head and went after Robbie who was climbing the wide staircase.

On the way home Tyrone said, "You know there is something familiar about the driver of that moving truck but I can't figure out what it is."

Lying beside my sleeping husband that night I began to shiver. What if Tyrone figured out who Robbie looked like? What if Bernie saw my son and I together and figured out that he was Robbie's father? I went looking for the whiskey to calm me down and help me sleep. The next morning I had a hard time waking up and Tyrone had to feed Robbie before he went to work. When he woke me at last I felt terrible.

"Why don't you take it easy today, Honey," Tyrone said. "Maybe you're getting the flu."

"I do have a headache," I told him sheepishly. "I'll take some aspirin."

Tyrone called me at lunchtime. "How are you feeling?" he asked.

"Oh, I'm fine Tyrone," I lied. "I think the aspirin chased away the flu. I'm cooking pork chops tonight. Will you be home about six o'clock?"

"I sure will, baby. See you then." He hung up.

The days flew by in a flurry of activity. Together, Tyrone and I chose the new carpet and drapes and arranged to have them installed. I was so busy that I almost forgot about Bernie and the WorldWide Movers until one sunny afternoon when I had just picked Robbie up from his nap and the doorbell rang. With Robbie in my arms, I went to answer it and there stood Bernie.

"Well, hello gorgeous." he said. "I knew it was you but I never had the chance to talk to you. And who is this little guy?"

"It's my son," I answered wanting desperately to put Robbie

down but he clung to my neck and Bernie moved closer to have a better look. I saw the light dawn in his eyes.

"How old is he?" he asked.

"He's two years old," I lied.

"He doesn't look like a two year old. My sister's boy is two and he's much bigger. I think this little boy is about a year old, add nine months to that and it's just about when you and I, um, you know."

"No, Bernie, you're wrong. This is Tyrone's son."

"It's funny, he has my widow's peak. Your husband doesn't have a widow's peak. This is my son, isn't it Jo?"

"No, Bernie. It can't be. It would destroy our lives. Think of the child." My voice held a desperate plea.

"No Jo, think of me. I think this is my son."

I put Robbie in his swing and came back to Bernie. "What do you want, Bernie," I asked.

He moved closer and began rubbing his hands up and down my bare arm. I shivered at the feeling of those well-remembered rough fingers. He held my arms and looked deep in my eyes.

"We were good together, Jo," he said as he leaned over to kiss me.

I pulled back but the butterflies were already fluttering in my stomach. "No, Bernie, I cried. My husband will be home soon. How will I explain you're being here?"

"I came to bring you the price of moving you into your new house."

"Please, leave it and go," I said, turning my back so I could not see the fire in his eyes.

"I'm not ready to leave," he said as he walked over to Robbie and bent down to talk to him. "Hi, little man. You're Mommy wants me to leave, but there's something I want before I go."

I walked over beside him. "What, Bernie, what do you want?"

"I want you to make sure we get this moving job done." I almost breathed a sigh of relief but he continued. "And I want to see you again."

"No, that's impossible. Tyrone would never forgive me."

Bernie smiled. "What would Tyrone do if he found out he was raising my son?"

The tears were running down my cheeks now. Bernie brought his rough fingers to my face and wiped them away with his thumbs.

"Don't cry, Jo," he said softly. "If you come to my room tonight, I'll leave you alone. After the move you'll never see me again."

"Do you promise me, Bernie?" I looked in his eyes.

"Sure, baby. I promise." He laid the moving bid on the table and went toward the door.

"Eight o'clock tonight. The Holiday Inn, Room 110. It's my

lucky number." He winked as he opened the door and was gone.

I went over and picked Robbie up from his swing. My heart was beating fast as I set him in his high chair and got a jar of baby food out of the refrigerator. I heated it in the microwave and took a baby spoon out of the drawer.

As I fed Robbie I began to plan how I could see Bernie tonight.

I finished with Robbie, wiped his face and laid him down with a bottle. I got out the hamburgers and French fries I had planned for supper and set the table.

When Tyrone came home I greeted him with a kiss and asked about his day. "Busy as usual," he answered washing his hands and sitting down at the table. "What's this?" he asked, seeing Bernie's bid beside his plate.

"Honey, you were so right to ask for a bid from WorldWide Movers. The driver brought it by today and it is the lowest one. And they will be able to move us on the fifteenth of next month."

"That's good. I can't wait to get into our new house."

"It will be great, Honey, and guess what, I saw the perfect table for the corner of the living room. I want to run down to the furniture store tonight and buy it. You don't mind watching Robbie, do you?"

"No, Jo you go ahead. I'm tired anyway."

At seven thirty, my knees trembled as I put on my coat and headed out the door. I parked in the far corner of the Holiday Inn lot so no one would see my car. Thank goodness the lobby was deserted and I hurried into the elevator.

Bernie opened the door and I slipped quickly inside. He looked so viral in jeans and a white shirt open at the neck.

"What do you want, Bernie?" I asked, trying to make my voice sound frosty.

He moved toward me and put his hands around my waist drawing me close. Our eyes met and I felt the old familiar heat in my loins, even though I tried weakly to push him away. The roughness of his fingers sent shivers down my spine. He kissed my neck while his fingers worked at the buttons on my blouse.

I did not stop him. "I think you remember how good we were together," he whispered removing my blouse.

"I really can't do this," I said.

Bernie led me into his bedroom where he continued to undress me. He stood looking at my naked body. "You are just as beautiful as you were two years ago," he said as he lowered me onto the bed. He quickly undressed. I tried not to watch as his muscular back and firm buttocks were revealed but my heart pounded as he climbed on top of me. My thoughts filtered back to the night we spent together and my arms crept around his neck. His rough fingers whispered over my skin. He sensed the awakening flames within me and his own passion mounted. The real world spun away and I was transported in a sweet agony of desire, made all the more desperate knowing it was the last time. I was ashamed at the magnitude of my own desire and I quickly rose, grabbed my clothes and went into the bathroom. I couldn't do it.

When I came out, Bernie was lying on the bed in his shorts. He looked so sexy and I tried not to look at him but I had to get his promise to leave us alone.

"Bernie, you've got to promise that you'll leave us alone."

"Don't worry, Baby. I won't even be here to move you. I'm going back to Pittsburgh tomorrow. I'm sure you'll do a much better job of raising the boy than I could. You be sure to take good care of him, you hear?"

"Oh, yes, Bernie, you know I will. This is good bye. Take care of yourself." I turned and hurried out the door without looking back.

I sat in the car and took some deep breaths, praying that Bernie would keep his word. I decided to tell Tyrone that the table I went to see was too big after all and I decided not to buy it.

When I got home there was a light burning in the living room but Tyrone was already in bed. I turned on the TV very softly and sat staring, not seeing what was on the screen. When my eyes grew drowsy, I turned off the TV and went to bed. I was with the man I needed to be with.

THE END

SWITCHED LOVERS
He Wanted To Share Me With His Twin Brother

As the lights went up, I gave my daintiest curtsy. My smile showered the up-lifted faces below me with love and adoration, which returned to me twofold. I realized all life was about change, but I couldn't fathom any other career outside of being a dancer.

Applause thundered fifteen minutes after my last solo. I bowed again. This time my arms were outstretched like wings, my right foot gracefully poised behind my bowed body. When the stage manager strolled onto the stage and stood beside me, a dozen red roses in his arms, I kissed my right fingers and tossed the kiss into the roaring audience.

Euphoria filled the air for ten more minutes.

"They love you," the manager whispered. "I've never seen an audience so hyped for a lead dancer. You deserve every whistle!"

Back in my dressing room, I placed the roses on my vanity and sighed with satisfaction. Another successful season was underway. In rare form, at the top of my career, I had willowy protégés begging for my time. Men sent roses after every show. Speaking engagements rolled in like waves. And to think, my face on the cover of high profile black magazines, and the countless dance magazines in the entertainment industry, but still, I was unattached.

Most times I couldn't believe it.

This current New Year had to be different. I prayed daily that some lovable brother would tap-dance his way into my heart and soon, or I'd be forced into retirement or embarrassment alone. I stripped, showered, and changed into black leather pants riding low under my diamond-studded navel, a pink feathery crop top, and stiletto black leather boots. I slipped large sterling hoops in my ears and up my wrists and looped a shiny dark dreadlock from my nape around my thick, waist-length ponytail.

Humming and admiring myself, I stared into the mirror and smeared Iman's luscious lipstick on my full lips. A knock on the door interrupted me.

"Miss Hall, are you dressed?" someone shouted.

Oh no! I thought. It was my agent. Somehow I'd completely forgotten our scheduled meeting.

"Sure, Dee," I called. "C'mon in."

A head full of raven curls peeped around the door. "Why am I hearing apprehension in your voice, Miss Dancing Diva?" Dee glared at me.

"Don't pretend you don't know," I chided. "When you didn't call me to remind me of the meetings, it was the last thing on my mind."

"You got another appointment I should know about?"

I shook my head. "I figured I'd holler at my folks at Spa Sharmayne in Riverdale. You know, treat myself to a facial and massage and a body wrap. Okay?"

In the mirror my svelte body sizzled in the sexy ensemble. The Spa Sharmayne staff loved to see it coming, especially the Hispanic woman with the pretty smile and the brother with the magic hands and the soft brown eyes everybody requested but rarely got.

Dee crossed her arms in an I doubt that manner.

"Miss Hall, sweetie, I'd like you to meet the journalist who is scheduled to interview you for the entertainment section of the Atlanta Journal. That, my dear, was the primary purpose of our meeting," she sighed. "This is a fabulous opportunity to create a standing-room only scenario for next month's run at The Fabulous Fox."

"Oh goodness," I moaned. How could I have forgotten? "Well, where is he?"

"On the stage."

"What are we waiting on, woman? Bring him back."

I outlined my lips and smeared cocoa butter lotion into my hands. Before I could organize my vanity, Dee returned. The finest man I'd ever seen followed her. Everything about the man captured my attention; his face, those eyes, the mouth, the broad shoulders, his height, the beautiful hands and stylish yet conservative attire. No doubt about it, I could truly fall, and hard, for a man like the one standing no three feet in front of me.

"Taylor Baldwin," Dee said eloquently. "This is Sunn Hall, the Jill Scott of the dance world."

He stepped forward, shook my hand. His touch soft but hard, I wanted this Taylor Baldwin to hold my hand and the rest of me forever. Without parting his lips, his eyes smiled. In that moment, I could have risen on my tiptoes and kissed his dark, enticing mouth.

"Nice to meet you," I said almost too eagerly.

"The pleasure is all mine, I assure you."

If only you knew, I mused.

"My brother and I love to see you perform."

"That's sweet." I tried not to get lost, permanently, in his eyes.

"Like the sun," he said, "do you hurt those who gaze too long in your eyes?"

"Sometimes," I said, thinking for a moment, then adding, "But like the sun, I shine on the worthy and the unworthy. Which are you?"

Ignoring my question, his eyes, consuming me, continued to glow, spreading a wicked warmth inside me wherever they roamed.

He turned to Dee. "Shall I conduct the interview here?"

She raised her brows, gave me a questioning stare. "Sunn?"

"Let's start here. Maybe a few pictures. Some conversation. Then we could finish the interview with me relaxing at Spa Sharmayne. That's where I was headed before Delores reminded me of our engagement."

Dee didn't seem to mind.

"If that isn't fine with you, Mister Baldwin, we can do everything here."

"No. Your plan is sufficient," he agreed, already unloading a recorder and camera.

Under Taylor's skillful questions and interview savvy, and the brightness of his flashing camera, I blossomed like an African violet, fresh and perfumed, rich and radiant. The sound of his voice, his intelligent quips, the penetrating way he stared at me when I answered his probing questions swept me off my black stilettos. On the ride across town, I couldn't help being turned on to his closeness on the back of Dee's big body black Benz. Whenever the car shifted, I fought not to slide into his long lean torso.

Inside Sharmayne's, Taylor's curiosity peaked.

"How often do you visit this place? It's so serene."

His camera snapped pictures of water flowing over rocks, of provocative nudes hanging on every wall, of the vast arrangement of decoratively wrapped gift baskets, of relaxation literature and movies, of brightly colored soaps and lotions, and of cosmetic displays.

"As often as it takes. I need this place to maintain loose limbs." His lips curled in a disbelieving half-smirk.

"Really," I added.

"Your man should help maintain your loose limbs."

"I don't own one."

His eyes smiled, and then he glanced around the corner into a steam room and shower. I stepped into an empty massage room and undressed. A white towel wrapped around my head and another draped around my body, I stuck my head around the open door.

"Tell you what, Mr. Baldwin. We'll come here together on my next visit. My treat. That's the only way you're ever going to truly know how fab these folks are."

Taylor's eyes softened. "Yeah, we'll see," he said offhandedly. I could tell he wasn't impressed.

"You want to stay while Gina does her thing?"

A brown-skinned woman with jet-black hair and a wide red mouth walked up and shook Taylor's hand.

I winked at her. "She's the best in the house."

"No thanks." Taylor began packing his camera. "That's a wrap tonight. I've got enough footage and material to collect a Pulitzer." He shook my hand. "It was nice meeting you, Miss Hall."

"Please. Call me Sunn."

"Okay, Sunn," he said, straight-faced and emotionless.

I didn't expect to hear from Taylor Baldwin, since he didn't appear to be a woman-chaser. Then again, I wasn't into calling brothers, who didn't fall prone at my feet upon our introduction, so I willed him out of my senses. It was hard but I managed. My demanding schedule with the Jonell Jameson Dance Troupe helped, considering it taxed my mind, body and soul. I didn't have a chance to think about Taylor, let alone men, in general.

Until on Friday afternoon, two weeks later, when Dee invited me to her office for a surprise and let the name I thought I'd forgotten roll off her tongue like honey. She was sitting behind a desk in her artsy, high-rise, downtown Atlanta office.

"Sunn, see anything new on my walls?"

I surveyed the space admiringly. "Looks gorgeous, as usual."

Then I spotted the Atlanta Journal article with the half-page photo of me on stage at the Fabulous Fox.

"Oh goodness," I gasped. "When did it come out? It's beautiful!"

Dee opened a desk drawer. "Here, Miss Dancing Diva. Congratulations on providing us with such good press."

The mahogany-framed article would be perfect in my study.

"Thanks, Dee!"

She stood and came around the desk to receive my appreciative hug.

"Could I get one of those?" The voice behind me caressed my back and sent shivers down my spine. It couldn't be? Could it? I thought.

Dee grinned. "He is the second part of the surprise."

Rooted to the carpet, I couldn't move but my body hollered. "Hell, yes!" He walked into the office and obliged me. The chemistry of our joined bodies was explosive.

"Would you like to have dinner with me tonight?" He smelled good enough to lick. "I've thought of you often and would have called but my assignments took me out of the country."

Red leather should be illegal on a brother this fine, I thought. He looked as if he should be on stage, in somebody's floodlight, and I'd be happy to make it mine.

"I'll be ready at seven," I said. "My address is…"

His raised finger interrupted me. "Dee gave it to me." He and Dee exchanged winks. "Gotta dash. Another appointment."

Taylor chose an upscale restaurant in Midtown. We received star treatment upon stepping out of the car, the valets Johnny-on-the-spot, which meant Mr. Baldwin had to be a regular. An attractive blonde led us to a cozy corner of the posh maroon space and presented a menu of delectable dishes.

Over red wine and dinner, I did what I feared got lost in Taylor's velvety soft eyes and easy conversation. His intriguing chatter whisked me to exotic settings he'd visited, making me feel as though I'd vicariously shared all that he described.

I even adored the way he flirted with the cute waitress, who relished his attention greedily.

As we were returning to my downtown condo, I didn't want the night to end.

"You busy tomorrow?"

His sexy 'you-must-want-me-to-come-in' smile almost made me shame.

"Yeah."

I pouted. "I understand. I am too, really."

At the door, I expected him to kiss me on the cheek and hurry away. Instead he waited for me to enter, then closed and locked the door behind us.

"I thought…"

"I know what you thought," he grinned devilishly. "I didn't say what I'd be doing; I simply said I'd be busy enjoying your company." He licked his lips. "Is that okay?"

Was it ever?

Taylor's presence sent me down a river of pleasure to a destination from which I desired no return. He moved slowly, kissing and murmuring his desire, his touch bringing fire to my long dormant regions. I usually enjoyed undressing a man, but I couldn't indulge in watching the slow exposure of his delicious sienna-colored bulk since I didn't want to stop feeling the full weight of him against my bare, burning body.

"Turn over," he commanded gently.

The sensation of lips on my back drove me out of my mind with longing. He knew just right where to kiss, press, lick, stroke. He brushed my long locks to the side and sent me off into dreamland with sweet strategically planted kisses.

"Taylor! Taylor!"

I didn't know how to tell him to please stop torturing me, to please strip and journey with me to paradise.

"Taylor," I repeated.

"What?"

"Please."

"What you got for me?"

"Anything you want."

"Yeah," he said, grazing his fiery fingertips over my body, as he peeled out of his clothes. "That's what I wanted to hear baby girl."

Finally nude, he wrapped me in his silky smooth embrace and I climaxed just anticipating the thickness of his dangerous joystick. We throbbed like a pulsing red light. I moaned. Stifled a scream. Bit my lip. I scratched his glistening back. He slipped on protection, and we became one, after what seemed like hours of foreplay. I clutched Taylor, my legs encircling his tapered waist, and whimpering like an animal, I rocked him into another world.

"You are so beautiful," he whispered against my ear.

I managed a smile. "So are you."

Whatever he wanted, I knew I'd give, I told myself. Whatever.

"Please stay?" I begged.

Sweat on his forehead, Taylor, a considerate lover, waited until I caught my breath, then led me back to the heights of passion again. This time with his hands and lips. The next time with other parts of his fabulous anatomy. I trembled with joy. Hours later, we climaxed for the hundredth time and fell asleep, exhausted and elated.

The next morning the aroma of breakfast almost made me fall out of bed. Could a brother that fine and intelligent be so well rounded? Hopefully, he was the one! Surely nothing about him would jump out and bite me when I wasn't looking.

I sat up and sniffed scrumptious smells.

My tummy growled after our night of love. Whiffs of sausages, cheese eggs, buckwheat pancakes and freshly juiced fruit pushed me to the vanity. By the time I heard footsteps on the stairs, I was brushed and refreshed, hungry for food and him.

"Morning, baby girl."

He'd found the golden tray and placed it on the reading table before me. Saturday sunshine streamed through my lacy curtains. The room felt complete, with this perfect man in absolutely nothing, a savory meal, and me in a pink Frederick's of Hollywood teddy.

"Good morning," I sang. "It smells great. Can't wait to dig in."

He grinned. "Not before I join you. I'll be right back."

Watching him leave the room, muscles rippling, thighs toned, butt rock-hard, I nearly had another climax. He has got to be mine, I told myself. My eyes closed and my hands clasped reverently.

Truly I could be his one desire.

Taylor spent the rest of that wondrous weekend with me.

If I thought he was the lion's roar between the sheets, he was Mr. It everywhere else. The brother could dance on skates, kiss through a movie and never miss a scene, jog in the park, swim, recite black love poetry, and give a full-body massage that rivaled Gina's at Spa Sharmayne's.

I cringed the closer it got to Sunday night. Like I anticipated, he got a call on his cell after brunch and from what I could make out, he had an assignment that would take him away for a two-week stint. And no matter how much I whined and pouted, he kissed me good-bye and promised to call as soon as the plane landed.

Dee claimed meeting Taylor Baldwin was the best thing that ever happened to me. She said I danced with a renewed intensity. I told her it was the fervor of passion. My mind whispered to my body one message; Dance your way back into Taylor's arms. Back into Taylor's arms.

Something readied me for the infrequency of his calls, although I ached to hear his voice. Maybe, I thought, absence makes the heart fonder, like the old saying goes. But-did he have to be that absent?

Before I met Taylor, I enjoyed an active social live between performances and practices and traveling. It was nothing to catch me partying at Club Jaguars or hanging tough at star-studded galas around the ATL. In his absence, I haunted the rooms of my condo eating and exercising and reading and analyzing dancers on music videos.

Two weeks later, on a Sunday evening, Taylor called.

I was so happy I nearly cried.

He said he missed me, wanted me to spend the next three days-if I could take a mini-vacation from the dance studio-with him in his personal space.

With the mobile phone still on my shoulder, I sailed about my bedroom, snatching and packing. This was the moment I'd been waiting for. If he weren't careful, I'd be with him before he could hang up the phone.

He lived on the third floor of an elegant apartment complex in off of the highway. Outside his bachelor's pad, the sky was alive with sparkling sunshine, the top of trees, and the songs of birds. On Monday, in his kitchen's bay windows, we enjoyed a hearty breakfast. Afterwards, Taylor and I ran the nature trail winding into the woods encircling his huge complex.

We rented Blockbuster movies later and held one another's feet for sit-ups as we laughed through several comedies. Since his bathroom boasted a Jacuzzi, he prepared an arrangement of white-chocolate dipped strawberries and helped me into warm scented bubbles.

"This must be what heaven is like," I said, accepting a strawberry from his fingers.

"No, Sunn, this is heaven right here on earth."

"Oh."

"And it gets better."

Somehow I didn't believe that, but I was willing to find out.

Taylor unwound my dreadlocks from where I'd wrapped them about my head like a scarf. He watched them cascade to the water's surface, where their tips disappeared under the colored water. Then as gingerly as if I was his baby, he began washing my hair and massaging my scalp.

"Oh goodness," I moaned. "That feels too good."

"Glad you like it. I love pampering my lady."

A question burst inside me. If I didn't voice it, I'd die.

"Am I your lady?"

Taylor turned me around to face him. "If," he looked me straight in the eyes, "you think you can deal with who I really am."

What, I asked myself, was the right next thing to say?

"Are you saying what I'm seeing and having seen is not who you really are?"

"I am what you've witnessed, and much more."

That sounded safe to me. Shucks, most of the brothers I'd encountered in the past year didn't hold a candle to what I already knew about Taylor Baldwin. Come what may, I was willing to turn the corner with Mr. Perfect.

"Tonight," he whispered, his hands slipped under the water to stoke fire in my love nest, "We'll see if what I got, you still want." I quivered all over when he nibbled my earlobe. "Remember what I said when we first made love?"

I nodded, trembling under the heat of the memory.

"Good. Tonight is the night for opening performances, of which you are the reigning diva, correct?"

My brows furrowed, but I smiled and mouthed correct anyway.

We made passionate love in the Jacuzzi-a thing I'd never done before. I felt unleashed, free, desired. When we rose from the cool water, we were ready for lunch, for which we dressed, a commendable Chinese restaurant, he said, not too far from the complex.

That night, towards eight, I got the biggest shock of my life. I didn't want to believe my own eyes, and the last time I checked my vision and it was still 20/20. Taylor had a twin! He was standing in Taylor's living room, caressing my hand, an identical sexy grin making that handsome face even more handsome. Still disbelieving, I stared from Taylor to his mirror image in the doorway.

"Sunn Hall, I'd like you to meet my brother, Baylor," Taylor announced.

I said nothing for a split second, and Baylor's laughter filled the awkward moment.

"Hi, Sunn." He extended his hand. "A pleasure to finally meet you. My brother and I have imagined what it must be to meet you for some time now. Gee, you're lovely."

He and Taylor hugged, and then Taylor hugged the pretty cinnamon-colored woman at his brother's side.

"Sunn, this is my lady, Dr. Lea Bell," Baylor said, his face aglow with pride.

I stared; not knowing which one was the most attractive.

"It's Lea." The curly-haired vixen looked like she could be a member of my dance troupe. She possessed a sense of presence. Charm.

"My pleasure," I smiled.

She floated in and perched on the circular sofa. "I caught your last show."

"The best in the ATL," Taylor quipped. "and please don't get too comfortable, Lea, as we're all going out."

Their playful banter drew my attention, although I wasn't jealous. I liked her instantly, and I found myself enveloped in conversation with Baylor and Lea. We laughed and talked like old friends. Both were well versed on the city's cultural scenes and certainly well read. Dining with them and Taylor was like sitting at Oprah's table for one of her televised book club dinners.

The dinner over, we partied at the Limelight, a nightclub in which beautiful women danced in cages hanging from the ceiling and crocodiles swam over rocks beneath the glass dance floor. Many drinks, much laughter and sensuous conversation later, morning arrived, and we were headed back to Taylor's apartment. He said we could chill out and enjoy nightcaps.

"Why don't you ladies change into something more comfortable," Taylor suggested, when we were settled in his living room.

"Yeah," Baylor piped up. "I'll see if Bro has any new movies in his collection."

Lea smiled. I followed her into Taylor's guest bedroom. Inside, I discovered that she and Baylor had a few articles of clothing in the closet and in the bottom dresser drawer. She slipped into a sexy two-piece lounge number, and I chose my black fitted one-piece jumper. Lea put her hair up and played with my locks, until she settled on two heavy ponytails above my ears.

"I look like a Rasta poodle," I giggled, looking in the bedroom mirror.

Lea laughed. "No you don't. You're too sexy, so come on."

We reentered the living room to find the twins in their pants and socks, no shirts or t-shirts. They looked like identical boxes of chocolate treats. With girlish giggles, Lea and I strolled to the round sofa where we fell into our lover's embrace, Lea knowing what I would soon learn.

For a long while the sound of our kisses filled the air. Then the guys got serious and the major action began. Totally unaccustomed to making love before another couple, I drew back. Taylor, sensitive to my emotions, stroked me and told me how attractive I was and reminded me of my former promise.

Gradually, under his kisses and reassurances, I yielded my apprehensions and allowed him to take me where he wanted me to go. In one smooth motion, he peeled me out of the black jumper and, while kissing every inch of me, came out of his pants and kicked them to the hardwood floor.

"Oooh Taylor," I moaned, unable to stop myself from begging, "please don't stop."

The man had to be the best lover I'd ever known.

I could feel him teasing me before I recognized the mischievous glint in his eyes. In a frenzy, I bit his shoulders and neck and earlobes. I whined wantonly. I tightened my steel grip on his thighs and back. But still he drove me continuously to the peak of climax, then eased me back, like a yo-yo. When I could take it no longer, or I would scream to the top of my lungs, Taylor tongued my navel ring and slid away from me.

Paralyzed with longing, I stiffened, my head tossing and turning, my body aflame.

Taylor reached for Lea, who favored a well-endowed rag doll, comfortable in his embrace. I would have hollered if Baylor had not eased his magnificent physique onto my seething body.

At first, jealous, my arms lay limb at my sides, my mouth a firm line. I jerked to see what I could see of Taylor, my Taylor, making love to Lea. Then Baylor held me, his cologne somewhat different from Taylor's, his skin cool and hot simultaneously. Against my will, my body welcomed him.

He whispered what sounded like French in my ear. I discovered his kisses where different from Taylor's. And he felt different yet similar. But he fit my contours like the perfect puzzle piece.

"If you want me to stop," Baylor murmured, slipping on protection, "say the word now, and I'll never touch you again." He looked into my eyes, and I realized that he thrilled me as much as Taylor did. "I'll never hurt you, little Sunn. I promise."

My heart and arms and legs and lips answered him for me.

"I love you too," he went on. "We've both loved you for a long time."

Thus said, we made crazy mad passionate love, until Taylor reclaimed me.

I decided not to share my newfound romantic situation with Dee, who finally reached me on Thursday afternoon, when I arrived home. Not very many people, especially my sisters I knew, on or off the stage, would understand what I had experienced with the Baldwin twins. For starters, I barely understood it myself.

And truly Dee would not have been able to conceptualize the experience of the two couples, our foursome, loving one another as intimately as we did. And that included a tryst between Lea and me, for our pleasure, not so much for Taylor and Baylor's, who did not complain.

Before I returned to the dance studio on Thursday evening, I lay on my bed and recorded as much of the experience as I could in my journal. Although I knew I was no longer appalled at desiring two brothers simultaneously, I didn't know how long we'd all be able to continue enjoying what we started. And if ever the day dawned when I wanted out, or any one of the others, I wanted to have everything in black and white. The experience was straight fiction and might garner me big loot, when I felt distant enough to reflect on it. And maybe even write about it.

I knew what I was doing could be considered morally wrong. And one day I would have the courage to end my liaison. Until then, I would relish the door I'd opened.

THE END

OFFICE SEX
He Had Me Addicted To
Love In The Afternoon

The phone jangled and I answered, "Medical Research, LaToya speaking."

"LaToya, I'm on my way over with the new Chief of Oncology," my boss, David said. "Remember, he's transferring his huge research project here and I need you to take very good care of him."

"Don't I always?"

"Yes, but—" my boss trailed off.

"If I'm not tough on all the research investigators, this hospital wouldn't have gone eleven years without one bad evaluation in all the surprise audits and inspections we've had. Someone has to be the watchdog."

"I know. But I fear this one's going to be a handful."

Fifteen minutes later, David introduced me to Dr. Calvin Greggs. I stared into heavenly deep gunmetal gray eyes with black lashes that any woman would kill for. His freckled light brown skin begged to be touched.

He was one fine brother.

For an instant I let my gaze drop to his mouth. Kissable popped into my head. I shook it as if I could get rid of those thoughts—thoughts about a man I'd never imagined having again.

I anticipated running my hands down his stubbled cheek, feeling the hard muscles in his chest, brushing my lips against his. Shock straightened my shoulders and I backed up a step. We were too close. It was getting hard to breathe.

For a moment I thought my heart would pound out of my chest. I cleared my throat and took a deep breath trying to regain control over my body's reactions.

After introductions, I was alone with Dr. Greggs and I gave him my usual stern lecture about consent forms and the way this University's Medical Center handled them.

"That's not the way I maintain my files," he said in a no nonsense tone.

"No disrespect, Dr. Greggs, but I don't care how you managed your files in San Francisco, but here we do things my way—the right way. I don't bend an inch on these rules for anyone, not even the Chief of Oncology."

Calvin stared me down, and I stared right back—right into those delightfully charming eyes.

"You don't intimidate easily, do you LaToya."

"No. I can't if I'm going to ensure that this is the tightest run Research Facility in the country. I don't want our facility making headlines unless it's stating we've just discovered the next miraculous cure for some fatal disease."

He smiled and my blood warmed.

His proffered hand startled me, but I let him take mine in his and the jolt that trailed up my arm straight into my heart made me pull back causing me to lose my balance.

He grabbed me by the waist. "Are you all right? he asked as he placed two fingers on my wrist. "Your pulse is beating very rapidly."

I could have sworn he said it with a knowing innuendo behind the words. He knew the effect he was having on me—and I believed his male-driven ego loved every minute of it.

I pried myself from his grasp, straightened my dress and said, "I'm perfectly fine. Now, if you don't have any further questions, here are the keys to your lab. I have work to do."

"What, no guided tour?" he asked.

"I'm sure you know your way around a lab."

"And a lot more," he whispered as he exited my office.

I slumped into my chair and rested my head in my hands. I tugged the top drawer of my desk open and I pulled on the photo I had hidden underneath the pen and pencil tray. I stared into dark brown haunting eyes. My heart hitched and the backs of my eyes stung.

It'd been three years today that my husband, Jamal, had died suddenly of a heart attack. Three years that had gone by achingly slow. Jamal stared back at me. Guilt flooded my being.

Then a voice echoed, "It's time to let me go."

I swung around in my chair to see who had come into my office. I was alone.

It amazed me that it only took a week for Calvin, as he insisted I call him, to settle into his lab. His goal was to find the cure for ovarian cancer. Too many women died from that disease every day. My mother died from ovarian cancer. That made his research even more important, to me anyway.

Even though we had gotten off to a rocky start, I looked forward to the daily banter we exchanged. A knock on my office door interrupted my thoughts.

"LaToya, I have a couple of orders that need to be placed. Have my funds been transferred from Memphis yet?"

My gaze traveled the length of him and I noticed his did the same. "You're working awfully late. I thought I was the only one here."

"I was at the medical school most of the day. I need to get some work done tonight. I have cells that need tending to or they will die—then where will my research be?"

"Leave me the orders and I'll check on the money. If it isn't here yet, maybe I can make arrangements to place the orders and pay when the funds are finally transferred."

"Thanks, you're a gem."

He turned and left and I didn't stop watching his tight behind until he turned the final corner. It took nearly forty-five minutes, but finally I had managed to place his orders. I gathered my belongings and locked my office door. At the junction in the hallway, I looked right toward the exit door and then left toward Calvin's lab.

"The considerate thing to do would be to let him know that his supplies were ordered," I mumbled. Before I knew it, I was standing inside his lab.

He was working in the hood tending his cells when I cleared my throat. He swiveled in the chair. His legs were spread wide and I wondered if what I read in that body language book was right—that meant he liked to experiment sexually.

I finally found my voice. "Just wanted to let you know that I ordered your supplies. I borrowed from Peter to pay Paul, so to speak."

He stood and sauntered toward me. "Is anyone else in the building?"

I swallowed hard. "No, we're the last ones."

"Do you have a few minutes?"

I nodded; mesmerized by the way he looked at me.

He slipped my coat and purse from my arms and led me to his desk. Easily picking me up, he sat me on the corner of the oak monstrosity.

"I've waited a long time for you to come to me."

"I...I'm sure I don't know what you mean?"

"Oh, I think you do."

He nuzzled a kiss on my neck and I melted against his hard chest. My lips found his and we deeply explored each other's mouths. His breath was hot with sexual heat—his body exuding a sensual scent that sent shivers up and down my spine.

A pool of fire gathered in my lower abdomen and I knew that Calvin would be the only one who could put it out. His hands reached for my zipper and it was down to my waist before I could object.

I'd never even flirted at work, now I was having sex in one of the labs. I wondered if I was dreaming. This wasn't me. I didn't behave like this. I could lose my job. Calvin's research could be placed in jeopardy.

But I didn't care. I wanted him and I couldn't wait.

"I didn't lock the door. You better lock it," I said, common sense seeping through the sexual fog that had overtaken me.

"I don't want to leave you."

"I won't be comfortable until your lab is locked," I said as I pushed on his chest.

He hurried to the door, flipped the lock and then dashed back to me as he removed his lab coat, tie, shirt and unbuckled his belt.

In that short space of time, I knew what we were doing wasn't right. I started to scoot off the desk but he stopped me."

"Where are you going, baby. We're locked in. No one is here. No one will know."

"I'll know," I said. "This isn't right, Calvin. Not in the office."

He pushed my dress free of my shoulders then rained kisses along the line of my collarbone and down my chest. Then he pushed aside the black lace until he was able to take a nipple in his mouth. I clutched at taunt muscled, arms. It had been three years since I'd had any kind of sexual release—three long years. Even if this didn't lead anywhere, didn't I deserve to return to the world of the living?

As he suckled, I tugged my dress over my hips. I was so glad that this morning I put on "date" matching underwear. Had I secretly known something might happen? No, it's just that I'd worn pretty underwear almost everyday since I met this marvelous specimen.

He unclasped my bra and my heavy breast sprang free. He pushed books and papers onto the floor making room for us on his desk. Then he carefully leaned me back. His fingers trailed down my belly until he reached the junction between my legs. I screamed out has his fingers parted then plunged inside me. I was so ready for him that the mere touch sent shivers of an orgasm rippling through me.

But that was just the beginning.

He didn't stop until I begged him to. If he hadn't, some security guard surely would have heard my cries and we would have been found out.

Finally, what I'd been waiting for happened. He plunged deep inside me and we moved together in a rhythm all our own.

There was an urgency about him now. He wanted to experience all the pleasure he had ensured I'd enjoyed and I wanted him to know it too. We carefully rolled on the desk until I was on top and I gave it everything I had until he cried out in pleasure.

When we were through, I was sure he'd invite me to dinner, take me out for a drink at least, but he only feigned a need to get back to his cells and before I knew it I was out the door and on my way home—alone.

For two weeks we led a secret life every evening after the rest of the staff left. During the day we enjoyed our usual banter—he'd want to do something one way, and of course I'd have to let him know, in no uncertain terms, that it was my way or no way.

He seemed to love that I stood up to him. I guessed most of the people he dealt with, like the residents and medical students, quaked in their shoes at his mere presence.

But I didn't quake.

I held my ground until everyone left—then I melted into his arms. But we never saw each other outside of the research lab. I was beginning to think he was married.

Calvin was all I could think about. I wanted so badly to ask him to my house for dinner. I wanted so badly for him to ask me out. But he'd shown no evidence that that would ever happen. He was the kind of man who probably had drop-dead women hanging on both arms when he went out. After all, he was a doctor—Chief of Oncology no less.

The phone rang and I picked it up on the third ring. "Medical Research, LaToya speaking."

"This is Brenda from Memphis Medical Research. I'm calling about Dr. Gregg's research funding."

"Yes, we've been waiting for the transfer for nearly a month. Do you finally have the transaction number?"

The woman on the other line did, and she gave it to me.

Thinking I was just casually ending the phone conversation, I said, "You must all miss Dr. Greggs very much."

"Like, hell. I'm glad he's gone. The man had no sense of ethics. He bedded every female who worked here, then made her life impossible. Most ended up finding other jobs, but I refused. I wasn't going to let him ruin my life."

My mouth fell open. That was the last thing I expected to hear. "You're kidding, right?"

"No, girlfriend, I'm not. Don't be taken in by his smooth talk. He'll love you and leave you, then make your life a living hell."

I quickly rang off and then sat staring at the telephone. Was it true? Was he really like that?

The buzzer rang letting me know that someone was at the entrance door. I insisted that the Research Building be kept locked at all times since Research is a multi-million dollar business.

I could see through the window that it was Shawn, the florist deliveryman. Dr. Macy White received flowers from her husband every third day or so.

New love.

How I longed to experience that just one more time in my life. Thirty-eight wasn't that old. I had a lot more years to live. And I'd realized since I heard the voice that it was time to let Jamal rest in peace and for me to move on. It was time to open my heart to love again.

The problem was the man I wanted to open my heart to might just be trouble.

I opened the door. The floral scent wafted past me, intoxicating me a bit. It was so overpowering. The dazzling colors. The huge variety of flowers. I couldn't begin to name them all. It was the largest arrangement Dr. White had ever received.

It was magnificent.

"I see Dr. White has another flower delivery, Shawn."

"Not today, LaToya. They're for you," Shawn winked and grinned so wide that his brown eyes twinkled.

"For me?" I asked stunned.

"Yes, and I can't think of another person who deserves them more. I'm so glad to see you're finally back in the dating game. You are one fine sister. You ought to have love in your life again."

I signed for the flowers and kissed Shawn on the cheek, thanking him for the kind words and wonderful bouquet. Stepping back inside my office, I saw David sitting in my chair with his legs propped up on my desk and his arms folded behind his head.

"You like?" he asked.

"They're from you?" I asked, stunned.

"Yes. You deserve them, LaToya. You're doing a fantastic job here. I'd like to take you to dinner tonight if you don't have plans."

My heart fluttered. Had I heard right? Was he asking me out? I'd never thought of David in that way. Of course I'd never thought of anyone that way since Jamal died until Calvin changed all that. My face flushed. I didn't know what to say. Before Calvin had arrived, I would have said yes. He was sensitive, but a no nonsense kind of bother. He told you like it was, and treated women with the respect they deserved. But Calvin ignited a sexual passion in me that had been dead for a long time.

What would happen if I broke it off? But I had to break it off. Calvin was all wrong for me. He brought out an immoral side of myself that I never knew existed. I wasn't the type of person to have sex in the office—to risk losing my job and the respect of my co-workers that I've worked so hard to gain.

No matter my decision right now—I couldn't continue seeing Calvin. Our relationship had to change back to purely professional. It would take a lot of work to get back to that point, but I had no choice.

I couldn't risk this job.

"I'm sorry, perhaps asking you out was the wrong thing to do. I hope this won't hurt our working relationship," David offered.

"No, it won't. I want to go out with you. I have a few things I have to finish up. Can I meet you at your car in say, twenty minutes?"

"Perfect." He stepped toward me and at first I thought he was going to kiss me, which would have been totally out of character for David. But he brushed the back of his hand against my cheek, then turned and walked out of my office. That was David. A little show of affection was okay for the office, but nothing more.

Unlike Calvin who wanted to do it all at the office.

"I have to get out of here before he comes looking for me. Maybe if I'm just not available to him, he will quietly back off and this will be all over."

An hour later I was comfortably sitting across from David in one of the local seafood restaurants. Nothing fancy, just good food and better company.

David and I talked and laughed and had a good time. I really hated for it to end.

"You know, LaToya, I've waited a long time for you to be ready to date. I know how much you loved Jamal and how much you hurt when you lost him. But something has changed in you the last couple of weeks—I hoped that the change meant you were ready to start living again."

Heat rushed to my face. If I told David what had been going on, I could lose him before I really had him. If I kept the truth from him, we would start our relationship on a lie.

I didn't know what to do. I only knew that this was the kind of man I was meant to be with. Passion fizzled, but love lasted. If Jamal taught me anything the short time we were together, he taught me that.

"I am ready, David. I ready to be with you. You're exactly what I need. But I don't want to jeopardize what we already have. Can we keep work and our relationship separate?"

"I think we can. It's not like we even work in the same building. You run Medical Research, not me. I only take the credit."

We laughed. A good, deep hearty laugh that made me warm all over.

"David, instead of taking me back to my car, will you take me home?"

His eyes became smoky with desire. His look sensually touched my heart and soul.

"Yes."

I had him wait until I had a chance to shower and slip into a negligee set I'd never worn. It was red and lacy and very revealing.

When I finally emerged from the bathroom, David was already in my bed. I sat on the edge and stroked his freshly shaved cheek. I cocked my head quizzically.

"You're not the only one who wanted to be fresh the first time we make love. I used your guest bathroom."

The gesture touched me.

I bent down and kissed him. It was sweet and gentle and reached down and opened the door to my heart.

A gentle breeze brushed through the open window and the curtains danced on the wafting air of honeysuckle.

I stretched out beside him and he wrapped his arms around me. He ran his hands over the soft, silky fabric of my gown, and then slowly took it off. He explored my body with his warm hands and played with my nipple with the tips of his fingers.

All the while his gaze never left mine. We watched each other, held our souls in each other's eyes. I stroked his body, first his buttocks which were tight and round and oh, so sexy. Then I found his shaft— hard and wanting.

I reached for my night table drawer and pulled out a bottle of gardenia oil. I placed a tablespoon in my hands and straddled his body, sitting on top of him, and then proceeded to rub him with the scented oil.

Then he did the same to me.

We took our time getting to know each other. We didn't rush. We made sure each of us were satisfied ten times over, and then, and only then, he took me in one smooth stroke and our bodies were joined and wrapped in a cocoon of love making.

It was as if I'd come home. I'd never felt so complete, so at peace, so loved. And it was our first time. It was as if I'd been waiting for David all these years and didn't know it.

His pace quickened and so did my breathing. I moaned in sexual pleasure and then the release came swift and hard and rocked my body until I cried out in ecstasy. Then he let out a soft moan and was spent.

David didn't rush off. He cradled me in his arms all night long.

I never dreamed I could be this happy.

The next morning, David went home, showered and changed as I did the same, then came back and picked me up. At work, Calvin was waiting for me in my office. I was thankful that David didn't walk me in.

"Where the hell were you last night," he demanded.

"Calvin, we are not going to work," I said as I crossed to my desk and removed my jacket, and then slipped my purse in my desk.

"No one dumps Calvin Greggs."

"Oh, get over yourself. It was an office fling that should have never happened. You don't care anything for me; you just wanted sex. Well, now the sex is over. We're going to get back to a professional relationship."

Calvin stood up, fast and furious, and towered over me. My heart pounded. For an instant I thought he was going to hit me.

"If you're planning on claiming sexual harassment, you better think again, bitch."

I gasped. No one had every spoken to me in that manner before. I knew I'd brought it on myself by making a very poor judgment. But I couldn't let him get away with it if I was going to regain my respect and dignity.

"Don't you ever speak to me in that tone or call me that name again. I don't plan on saying anything to anyone about our sexual encounter—quite frankly I just want to forget the whole thing. Now get out of my office."

He didn't budge for several minutes, and it took all my strength not to let my gaze break from his. I had to hold my ground. I couldn't let him see how much he got to me.

Finally, he turned and left my office. I fell into my chair, my knees shaking like jelly. I swallowed hard as Dr. White walked into my office. Had she heard our argument?

I felt the blood drain out of my face. My stomach flipped flopped and I thought I would be sick. I didn't want anyone to know what I had done. I was so humiliated.

"Good morning, Dr. White," I finally managed. "Can I help you with something?"

"I just brought you a new list of the human subjects that are participating in my research project."

I stood to meet her, and took the offered piece of paper from her hand. "Thanks. The consent form review begins next week. I appreciate the effort."

She eyed me in a way she never had before. I didn't think it was my imagination.

"You're welcome."

When she walked out of my office, tears stung the backs of my eyes. If she knew, within days the whole department would know. As much as I liked Dr. White, she was a gossiper. She wouldn't keep something this juicy a secret.

I had to tell David before someone else did.

David had agreed to come to my apartment for dinner that night. When he arrived, I knew he had found out about Calvin.

"Please don't look at me that way, David, please give me a chance to explain."

"I thought I knew you," he said as he slipped off his overcoat. I thought you were this one type of person and now I've learned that you're someone I didn't know at all."

"No, that's not true. I made a mistake—granted a very large mistake—but you have to understand. If that hadn't happened, I might still be trapped within my grief and not able to move on with a relationship with you."

"We don't have a relationship. Not anymore. I can't condone what you did."

I chewed on my bottom lip. I couldn't believe I'd lost him. Within twenty-four hours I went from being the happiest I've ever been to complete and total devastation.

"David, if you aren't going to at least hear me out, why are you here?"

"I guess I just wanted to know if it was true. If you had really not only slept with Calvin, but at the office. At the office!"

"You're right, there is no excuse. What I did was inexcusable. But I thought you were a forgiving man. Can't you even try to understand how—" I broke off. "I don't even know how to justify it. There is no justification. All I can say is that I love you, David. I love you more than I ever loved Jamal. You may think that's a crock of bull since we've only had one night together, but I know. Last night was the best night of my life. Nothing—I mean nothing—can compare to last night. Surely you felt it, too."

"I did. That's why learning about you and Calvin—" it was his turn to break off.

"Hurt and shocked you?"

"Yes," he said then sank down to the overstuffed chair.

"All of Medical Research knows now, don't they?"

"If they don't by now, they will by tomorrow."

"It isn't that you can't forgive me, you can't stand the humiliation, isn't it."

"Can you? Can you go on working there?"

"Yes. And I'll tell you why. Calvin Greggs did this very same thing to several other women in Memphis. Most of them just gave up their job, but one of them filed a sexual harassment suit. That's why he moved his research here—it's not because of the smoke he blew up your butt. He was running away.

"I'm not going to let him beat me. He's not going to win. I'm going to keep my job. I'm going to regain the respect I've lost if it takes years. He will not win. And if you give us up, you will let him beat you. Is that what you want, David? Do you want Calvin Greggs to take away the happiness that we found together? Do you want him to be the big winner? I thought you were better than that. I thought you fought for what you believed in, for what you wanted, for what was right.

"I'm willing to fight for us, are you?"

I pulled him to his feet. "If you're not, leave."

He stood there watching me for several minutes—it seemed a lifetime. My heart stopped, waiting for his response. I was terrified that I hadn't gotten through to him. That I'd lost my one chance of happiness since Jamal's death.

Finally he said, "Let's get a bite to eat. I want people to see us together tonight."

My heart finally started beating again. I knew it would take time, but I never give up. I would regain the respect of my colleagues again. And David and I would make it happen together.

THE END

LYING WIFE
My Ex Made Him Jealous!

After my husband Stephen's speech everyone applauded, I sat at the table alone, and watched him at the podium. I was happy for him but felt a little empty.

I watched as people stopped to talk to him and he began to make his way back to where I sat. This was a big night for him because he was being honored for opening his second car dealership.

It had been a long hard struggle with a wife and three babies, but against all odds he made it. Now the children graduated from high school, were away at college, and it was Stephen and me alone in a huge house that sometimes seemed to swallow us.

Stephen came back to the table looking both excited and triumphant. He sat next to me and gave me a kiss on my cheek.

"I'm very proud of you. Congratulations," I said.

"That means a lot coming from you, Celeste. All I've ever wanted was to give you what you wanted."

"You have," I said.

Bob Stephenson rushed over to the table, asked if he could borrow Stephen for just a minute, and I said yes. I sat with two other wives and conversed with them.

After we left the party, Stephen drove around to pick me up, and I jumped in. I held my hand on his as he shifted to second gear in his corvette.

"Stephen, why don't we drive by the beach like we used to when we first met?" I wanted to do something romantic because I was extremely bored with my marriage. I loved Stephen but he was just too serious about his business.

"We were just kids then," he said.

"I know, but. . ."

"But, we're not kids any more."

"Your right we're not, but I wanted to make love to you on the beach."

"We can make love at home in our bed," he said.

He drove into the drive way, and put the corvette in the garage. I went into the bedroom, changed my clothes, and put on a sexy silky black negligee. I took the wine out of the refrigerator, and poured two glasses.

"Want a glass of wine?"

"Sure." He looked at me and took the wine.

"Don't you notice anything?" I said.

"Of course I do. Come here."

He pulled me into his arms and I fell into his lap.

I took his hand and led him into the moon lit bedroom. His hands held my waist and held me close to his chest.

He lowered his mouth to mine, with wanton and force. He let his tongue trail down my chin and the curve of my throat.

I turned my back to him so that I could turn down the comforter on the bed. I felt the hardness of his body behind me, he touched my inner thigh, lifted me slightly in the air, and then I fell into the bed. Stephen began to touch me, over the years we had been together he knew all the right moves, where his fingertips tickled, rubbed, and pressed.

I unbuttoned his shirt and ran my hands over the short curly hair on his chest. He lowered his mouth to mine while his hands never left my body he pulled off my negligee and panties. In the darkness he removed his shirt, threw it, unbuckled his belt, and his pants fell on the floor. He put my breast in his mouth and sucked gently.

My hands roamed his body finding his length, guiding, and opening to a fiery embrace. When he plunged into me I wrapped my legs around him and matched his rhythm until we took each other.

The next morning at breakfast Stephen was reading the newspaper and drinking a cup of coffee.

"My high school reunion is next week," I said.

"Is it?" He said, and never looked up at me from the newspaper.

"Stephen, I told you two months ago. You said you'll try to get away with me."

"Oh, I forgot," he said.

"Can you?" I said.

"Can I what?"

"Go to my high school reunion. We've discussed this already don't you pay any attention to me?"

"Of course I do," he said.

He looked up blankly, put on his suit jacket, and kissed me. "No, baby it's no way that I am going to be able to go."

"Why not?"

"I have to work that's why."

"Stephen, you are the boss."

"So what, I can't put my business on hold because you want me to go to some silly reunion."

"I thought when the kids were away at college we were going to spend more time together. Everything is business to you our relationship is not business, Stephen."

"You go."

"By myself?" I said.

"You won't be by yourself because I'm sure you sister and brother are going. You certainly have been wanting to see your parents."

"I don't believe this, what is your problem? You don't want to do anything together anymore. Our last anniversary I kept our reservations and celebrated alone because you were to busy."

I just didn't know what his idea of love was anymore. It seemed when we were struggling to make ends meet we were in love now all Stephen cared about was making money. It hadn't always been this way, for the first few years were great with Stephen. I was a young mother of three, it had been hard, but we had each other. Stephen had been a dedicated father changing diapers, and getting up for two o'clock feedings. We would sit in our little apartment and just enjoy each others companionship. Our life then was perfectly romantic. As time went on Stephen began selling more automobiles and spending less time with me. He worked all day sometimes not getting home until late at night and I would be in bed.

I began clearing the dishes off of the table, and stacking the dishwasher. I slammed the door closed and turned it on. He stared at me.

"I'm doing this for you, Celeste. Do you think that I would be working this hard if I was in this alone. I want us to have the best of everything."

"Your doing this for yourself."

"That's not fair. I don't have time for this nonsense, I have to get to work. Call me when you get there and leave me the number at the hotel your staying in."

"Okay."

After Stephen left, I began pulling my clothes off hangers, and throwing them into my suitcase. I knew that Stephen loved me, but I was extremely frustrated with my marriage. I knew it sounded selfish but sometimes, I wondered what my life would have been like if I married my high school sweetheart. I planned to find out, and I hoped he would be at the reunion.

I finished packing my clothes, threw my suitcases in the trunk of my car and drove to my hometown.

For several days I sat around my mother's house just enjoying being back home with my parent's and siblings. I did call Stephen, but he wasn't home as usual. So I left a message of my hotel room number and my telephone number on the voice mail.

I tried putting my life into perspective and decided not to try and get in contact with Daryl Smith. I thought about him, although I tried pushing him out of my mind. I wondered what it would be like making love to him now that we were both grown.

Then one Sunday afternoon we were having dinner at my mother's and Daryl walked into the dinning room with my brother Troy.

"Celeste, there's someone that wants to see you," Troy said.

"Who?" I said.

He walked into the dinning room and was extremely handsome. The years seemed to do this man justice because he was totally fit, and a vision of strength.

"Celeste, I had to see you, and when Troy told me you were here I couldn't wait until the reunion."

"I'm glad you did," I said.

"Why don't we go an have a drink?" He said.

"Okay."

My mother gave me a sharp look, and I felt as if I was in high school again and laughed. I kissed her on her cheek and told her not to worry.

At the bar I ordered a glass of wine, he had a beer, and I found it hard to believe that I was sitting there having a drink with him after so many past years.

"What have you been doing all of these years," I asked.

"I'm a fireman and that keeps me very busy."

"Are you married," I asked.

"Sure."

"Why did you break up with me?" He said.

"Oh, that was so long ago I can hardly remember it myself," I said.

"Fair enough. Is your husband coming to the reunion?

"No, he thinks his business is more important than a silly reunion."

"I don't believe that," he said and took a sip of his beer. His eyes looked deeply into mine as if he were studying me. He seemed to look into the depth of my soul and I looked down into my lap. He reached across the table and grabbed my hand.

"It's the truth, do you know who I spent our last anniversary with?"

"No," he said.

"No one, because he couldn't leave his business deal, and I kept our reservations and celebrated alone."

He stood and pushed the chair back under table. "I better walk you back home," he said.

"Okay," I said.

We began walking back to my mother's and it consisted of a three block walk. We were walking very slowly as if taking a Sunday stroll. He grabbed my hand and I felt very close to him. I was not thinking about my problems with my husband Stephen anymore.

"I would never treat you like that if you were mine," he said.

"You wouldn't?"

"No, I want to make love to you, Celeste."

"I can't I'm married."

He came close to me and I felt his body press up to mine. We stood in the street a block away from my mother's house when he kissed me. I pulled away from him, but he moved forward and grabbed me around my waist.

A loud screeching noise from tires pulled up next to us and it made us stop kissing and look.

Stephen jumped out of the car and came around to where we were standing.

"Get your hands off of my wife," Stephen said.

"Stephen!"

I was in shock.

"What are you doing here?"

Stephen never answered me, but stormed over to Daryl and released a long straight left that caught Daryl flush on the chin. The other blow caught him in the eye and threw him clear across someone's grass. Daryl was too dazed to move.

I ran over to Stephen, grabbed his arm, so that he couldn't hit him again.

"Stephen stop it."

"Why should I? I saw what you were doing with him," he shouted. He was extremely angry. "Get in the car."

I got in the car and we drove away. At first I could not believe what had happened myself, how could something go wrong like this, I asked myself. I knew what I had been thinking in my heart but I had no intentions in hurting Stephen like this.

I never had an affair before, but the truth was, I came here thinking about what it would be like to make love with him, and I felt ashamed.

"I didn't do anything, nothing happened," I said.

"I don't believe you," Stephen said.

He said nothing to me at all, I looked over at him in the car and his jawbone was tight. He dropped me off at my mother's, I kissed her good-bye, got in my car, and drove home.

I went into my house and everything looked like it did when I left it. Stephen came in behind me without saying a word, walked to the bar, and poured himself a drink.

"Stephen, nothing happened."

"Is your life so bad here that you had to go and do this to us, Celeste?"

"No, Stephen it's not."

"I have to go," he said.

He grabbed his keys off of the table and slammed the front door.

The next day there seemed to be a void in me that felt it would be there forever. This was something that I didn't feel that I was going to get over, and knew that I couldn't keep saying to him that I didn't do anything. I honestly didn't know what to do at this point. The worst part was that the guilt didn't go away, it felt like I wore it around my neck, and I knew that Stephen had a right to be angry with me. I was angry with myself because I knew that I was married and I shouldn't have let Daryl kiss me like that.

That night Stephen didn't come home, I called his office, but he wasn't there.

The house was big and empty I looked around in the living room and it looked like a ice skating arena. It was big and lonely with furniture that sat around in dark corners of the room, Stephen had worked hard to give me all of this, and I betrayed him. It was as if I had to deal with the truth by myself and that I might lose my husband over this.

I loved Stephen. He had to understand that, I guess that I was felt lonely, and let Daryl move right into the depth of my loneliness.

I began to get worried about him when he didn't try to get in touch with me, so I called his cell phone.

"Stephen, where are you?"

"I'm at the Holiday Inn, if you need to get in touch with me here is the telephone number," he said.

He gave me the telephone number and I wrote it down with tears in my eyes. I could hardly see the paper because I was crying.

"When are you coming home?"

"What do you care."

When I reached my husband's hotel room I looked into his eyes when he opened the door, and he was very hurt. His eyes looked at me in a way I wouldn't wish on no one.

He stood in the door blocking my entrance.

"Can I come in?"

He stepped aside, "sure."

He looked good I hadn't seen him in a week, I wanted to hold him, and run my hands over the short curly hair on his chest.

I knew at the time when Daryl kissed me that it was wrong. I let the loneliness of the nights I spent alone waiting on my husband stand in the way making me weak of a gentle touch. How could I let that happen? I asked myself over and over.

Stephen was living in the Holiday Inn, what could I say that could take the hurt away from him, and how could I fill this large wedge that had the capacity to rupture our long term marriage?

"All the years we've been married and you don't believe me."

"I saw you, and my eyes don't lie to me."

"You didn't see anything."

"Your arms were wrapped around him, and you were kissing him." It was true my arms were around him, but I had been pushing him away from me. It was innocent and I wanted to keep it that way when Daryl had kissed me it had surprised me more than anything else.

"I want you to realize something about our marriage, I guess, I was feeling lonely because we don't do anything romantic anymore. I miss that part of our marriage."

"You were with someone else because your not getting any romance at home. Celeste I don't have time for this."

"I know you don't seem to have time for anything."

"I can't trust you," he said.

"You're trying to act like I had some steamy affair, and now you can't trust me. You are the problem, Stephen."

I tried to be patient and listen to Stephen, but it kept getting harder. His tone was sullen, cynicised, and condescending.

"You broke the trust," Stephen said.

"What trust," I said. I picked up my purse and walked toward the door. "Good-bye, Stephen." I really had enough of this and I felt that it was over.

My friend Nadia came to see me, and we embraced when she walked in. We had been friends since high school and remained very close.

"How are you feeling?" she asked.

"Fine."

"You can't tell me your feeling okay, because I'm your best friend."

"I know."

"It's over between Stephen and me, Nadia."

"I can't believe that," she said.

"Believe it, because I'm not about to stay married to a man that can't trust me."

The room grew silent a moment, and she touched my hand making me look at her. "You certainly got Stephen's attention this time," she said and laughed.

"What do you mean?"

"He's jealous that's why he's so angry. Most men that have been married a long time take their wives for granted. They just think that no one else will want her or find her attractive, but that's not true."

"I know," I said.

"Stephen just got a wake up call. There are a lot of couples that are in divorce court right now because the husband had an affair with another woman. But like my mom always said, 'they can dish it out, but they can't take it.'" We laughed.

"He's treating me like I had some steamy hot romance with Daryl and all I was trying to do was get that man off of me. Sure I thought about it, but I have never done anything like that to Stephen."

"Were going to have a good time at the reunion tomorrow night and you can take your mind off of all this."

"I'm not going to that reunion, Nadia."

"Why not?"

"All of this has given me a headache and I think I'm going to just stay home," I said.

"Oh, no your not. Your going to that reunion and we are going to have a good time," Nadia said.

"Okay."

Nadia had a way of making me feel better I should have a good time tomorrow night at my high school reunion.

After Nadia had gone home I thought about what she said, and maybe she was right. I did feel that Stephen was taking our marriage for granted thinking that I would always be there. I guess I had taken it for granted too thinking that he was not going to be there. He was always gone, and most nights I was alone.

The night of the reunion I had seen people that I hadn't seen in over twenty years, and Nadia and I had a good time gossiping about some of our classmates. I was happy that a lot of them was now successful or had wonderful photos of their children. But I was still upset about Stephen, there was a void in me, and I didn't know how to let it go.

"I hope that I didn't get you into too much trouble." I turned around and Daryl was standing next to me. He looked a little better than the last time that I saw him, but his eye was still swollen.

"How's your eye?"

"Better, but I could use a nurse to help me."

"Daryl, I told you that I'm married."

"I know I met him, remember," he said.

"How can I forget."

We laughed, someone was calling him, and I turned to look. He looked very frustrated when he saw a woman approaching him.

"Excuse me," he said.

"Sure."

He walked to her and she was very pregnant. I heard them talking and he was very mean to her. He told her that he didn't believe for a second that it was his baby and that she could leave him alone. She was very frustrated and told him that he knew that it was his. I shook my head in disgust. Everyone was staring at them as he stormed out of the hall, and she followed him. If I had had any fantasies about that man they were gone now, I laughed to myself.

I walked to the table and began making my plate of dinner when someone walked up behind me and kissed me on the back of my neck.

I turned around to look to see who it was, and it was Stephen.

"Stephen!"

"It's me, baby."

I grabbed him so tight, and he kissed me.

"What are you doing here?"

"I couldn't miss seeing my prom queen. I had to be here. You were right I have been a jealous fool, and I couldn't let that break us up."

"Me either."

"You can count on me to do everything that I can to keep this relationship, and if you want to make love on the beach or anything else that is what were going to do."

"Wait, I have something for you,"

"What?"

"I didn't know what color your dress was so I took a chance and bought you this," he said.

"It's beautiful," I said.

It was a corsage, and he pinned it to my dress. We danced the remainder of the night and I looked into his eyes.

Two hours later after the high school reunion was over Stephen met me at home. He stepped into our bedroom and I went to him. My hands were trembling but I ran them up over his chest. I unbuttoned his shirt so that I could kiss the short curly hair on his chocolate chest.

He grabbed my hips pulling me close to him, and his lips trailed over my chin to my throat.

We laid back in the cool sheets, and Stephen's fingers ran down my body. He raised himself on one elbow and looked at me. "What's wrong?" I said.

The room was dim, lit by a soft lamp on my side of the bedroom, I reached to turn off the light, but he grabbed my hand. "No, I want to look at you," he said.

He pulled me down, lowered his lips to mine, and I began to shed my clothes while our lips never parted. He began to touch my breast, ran his hands down further over my stomach to my inner thighs. His fingertips pressed, rolled, and gently tickled, until I was breathless.

He picked me up and held me in his arms and we kissed one last time. He struggled to get his clothes off. I opened up to him, and he entered my depth. He plunged deep, we rolled together, and I met his movements simultaneously. My hips rose and fell and I felt his hard body against my thighs. He held onto me tighter, plunging deeper, and took me fast. Then he buried his face in my hair as his body stiffened and we fell exhausted into each others arms.

Stephen jumped up, reached into his coat pocket, and stepped back over to the bed.

"I have something for you," he said.

"What is it?" I said.

"We are going to get away to this romantic place and make love on the beach."

It was tickets to a cruse of the Caribbean.

"How are you going to get away from work to do that?" I said.

"I'm the boss remember," he said.

"Yes, I remember."

I grabbed him, pulled his mouth to mine and kissed him. I was so happy that we were together and talking again. This time I planned to show my man that the years we spent together meant more to me than any fling that he or I could have ever had. We were going to keep our relationship exciting as the first time that we made love.

THE END

BACK DOOR LOVE
I Hid My Sex Life

"I wish you didn't have to go. Please stay at home with me," I begged. My husband gazed at me with his dark, compassionate eyes. He had recently grown a beard and mustache and he looked more handsome than ever.

"When we got married, you knew what our life would be like," he warned in his deep strong voice. I quickly turned away and shredded my tissue. I had been crying all morning. My husband was on his way to Italy for a business trip. He owned a large international company and he was always traveling on business.

When we first got married, I used to travel with him on his business trips. I was only twenty-two years old and I had seen most of the world. I'd been to France, Italy, Japan, and South America. However, I stopped accompanying my husband Mark on his business trips because I'd spend the entire time alone. He was always on business meetings, conference calls, and business lunches. He would always return to the hotel room after I had fallen asleep. I didn't like spending time alone in these foreign cities. I hated walking the streets while all of the natives spoke a different language. Soon I started to stay home. I didn't see the need to travel to these cities anymore. After all, I wasn't spending any time with my husband while he was on his business trips.

The airline employee announced the final boarding call for the flight to Rome, Italy. I hugged my husband as I continued to cry. His body felt tight and muscular beneath his charcoal gray business suit. My heart pounded and I became aroused with desire. Since my husband was gone all the time, he had not made love to me in two months. I craved his body the way I craved hot cocoa on a cold winter day. I felt neglected and confused and I just wished my husband would make love to me again.

"Oh, Mark, I'll miss you so much!" I cried. He kissed me long and hard with his full, beautiful lips. We had only been married for two years and I already felt like my marriage was ending. Mark was thirteen years older than me. I fell in love with him because he was rich, he owned his own company, and he could take care of me. I had grown up in a poor ghetto, and it had always been my dream to marry a rich man.

"Don't worry, Tina, I'll be back before you know it," he said. He squeezed my hand before he boarded the plane. I watched the plane take off into the sky from the large glass window.

I continued to cry as I drove my Black BMW to my large mansion. After I parked it in the garage, I ran inside. Our butler wanted to know if I wanted dinner, but I told him that I was too upset to eat. I cried myself to sleep that night, missing Mark desperately. Our marriage was so unreal. I was unhappy and dissatisfied. Even though we were rich, I found that money couldn't buy love and happiness.

The next day, while I was sitting out by the pool, I continued to think about Mark. I missed him and I wanted him home with me. I cried again as I thought about him. I then looked up and noticed a beautiful man cleaning our pool. He slowly pulled the large pole through the crystal blue water. His brown body looked sleek and shiny. He was wearing a pair of shorts and his legs looked strong and muscular. My mouth watered as soon as I saw him. He must have sensed that I was looking at him because at that moment he turned and looked at me, and our eyes locked. He quickly abandoned his task and walked over to me. I was completely mesmerized by this gorgeous man. "Hi," he said shyly. I was wearing my cranberry bikini, and the pool-cleaning man was giving my body the once-over.

"Hi," I replied as I tried to dry my tears. I noticed that he had a Jamaican accent. His voice was deep and smooth. He looked like he was about my age, and I was deeply attracted to him.

"I'm Gerald," he said.

"I'm Tina," I replied. He then told me that my husband had hired his company to clean the pool every week.

He touched my face. His hands felt kind and gentle. It had been so long since a man had touched me that way. "You look so sad. Why?" he asked softly.

I sighed and before I knew it, I was telling Gerald all about my marriage problems. A few hours later, after he had cleaned the pool, I found that I felt much better after talking about everything.

"You're so beautiful, Tina. Mark is a fool for treating you like this," he said. I was so thrilled when Gerald said I was beautiful. Mark had not complimented me in ages. It was nice to be admired again.

The following week, Gerald came to my house every day. He didn't have to clean the pool that often, but he came by to see me. He knew that my husband was in Italy, so he wasn't afraid of getting caught. We played water games in the sparking blue water of the pool. We ate watermelons and peaches under the shade of the exquisite trees in my backyard. My butler fixed us exquisite lunches of baked flounder and succulent crabmeat.

I soon found my feelings growing for Gerald. He was kind, nice, and understanding, but most of all, he made me feel like a beautiful woman. I wanted our relationship to last forever. He treated me better than Mark ever did. After Gerald had been visiting me for about a week, he showed up on my doorstep with a bouquet of red roses. I was so excited that I cried. It had been so long since a man had paid me so much attention. Gerald was wearing a pair of tight black jeans and a white tee shirt. "You look so handsome," I whispered as I inhaled the sweet scent of the roses.

I led him inside and we shared a long passionate kiss. So far, our relationship had been chaste, but as Gerald kissed me, I longed to have his body inside of mine. He tweaked my nipple with his finger and I shuddered with delight. I was wearing a red silk shirt, but I wasn't wearing a bra. I ached to have his hands touch my breasts again.

"You're a passionate woman, Tina. I like that," he growled in my ear.

"Let's eat," I said. My voice quivered with delight as I led him into the dining room. I looked great that evening. I wore a short skirt and high heels. I noticed Gerald staring at my legs as we sat down to eat. We feasted on grilled steak with baked potatoes. For dessert there was chocolate cake with vanilla ice cream. I watched Gerald's full beautiful lips as he enjoyed the tasty treat. My heart pounded with anticipation. I had not heard from my husband since he left for Italy, and for once I didn't miss him. I had Gerald in my life now. He made me feel safe. He made me feel free. He made me feel like a real woman.

"Oh, you're so beautiful, Tina," Gerald breathed as he took me into his strong arms. His skin was the color of dark cocoa and he smelled like musk after-shave. He caressed my neck as we kissed. Our tongues mated as my heart continued to pound. "Let me make love to you, Tina," he begged. I was so nervous that I couldn't find my voice. I merely nodded. Soon Gerald carried me up the stairs in his strong arms.

He lay me upon the bed. The white silk sheets felt good against my heated skin. He opened the window and the warm summer breeze blew into the room. He lit a vanilla-scented candle and soon the room was basked in the sweet smell. He slowly removed my shirt. He then placed his eager mouth over my nipple. Soon my breasts resembled large dark peaks. He then unzipped my skirt and removed my silk panties. He placed his finger over my special place and found that I was creamy and moist.

"Oh, my, you're so sexy, Tina," he cooed. He removed his clothes and I feasted my eyes on his gorgeous body. He was hard and solid as a rock. His dark body was rippling with muscles. He got a good workout each day from cleaning the swimming pools in our neighborhood. His organ was long and hard. He was so beautiful that tears came to my eyes.

"Tina, why are you crying?" he asked. His Jamaican accent suddenly became thicker and his dark eyes were full of compassion. "Are you upset because you're being unfaithful to your husband? We don't have to make love if you don't want to. I don't want you to feel as if I'm rushing you into anything," he said.

"Oh, Gerald. I'm crying because you're so beautiful. It's been so long since a man has paid so much attention to me."

"Oh, Tina, please don't cry." He licked my tears away with his long eager tongue. I then caressed his strong back and his shapely butt with my eager hands. He felt good and strong and I was glad that he was in my bedroom. He stroked my body with his hands like an expert. He toyed with my erotic zone with his nimble fingers and soon my high-pitched screams filled the room.

When he entered my body I groaned with pleasure. I felt like I was flying as high as a kite. Gerald made wild and passionate love to me. He loved me for a long time and my body felt quenched from his gentle touch. He screamed as he came and soon he fell on top of me. The warm summer breeze blew over our sweat-drenched bodies. I clung to Gerald as if I never wanted to let him go. "You're so pretty, Tina. You're the prettiest woman I've ever known and I'm falling in love with you." His deep voice was full of so many emotions that it brought tears to my eyes.

"Please don't cry again, Tina," he pleaded.

"I can't help it, Gerald. I'm so happy that I'm crying," I explained.

"You're so thin. You need to start eating more," he said. I'd been so worried about my marriage over the last few months that I had lost my appetite. So far, I'd lost twenty pounds. Gerald ran his fingers over my slim brown legs. He then pressed his finger into my belly button and I laughed. He ran his fingers through my long black hair. He chuckled and his dark eyes sparkled with delight. My heart pounded as I became aroused again. He ran his fingers all over my thin body and I quivered. I opened my legs and he entered me again.

"Oh, Gerald!" I whimpered with pleasure. He made love to me all night and when the sun was peeking over the horizon, we finally fell asleep.

I was abruptly awakened the next morning by the ringing telephone. "Hello." My voice was still groggy from sleep. Gerald clung to me with his strong arms.

"Tina?" I gasped when I heard my husband's voice. I heard people in the background speaking Italian, so I knew he was calling me from his office in Italy.

"Mark?" I whispered. Usually a phone call from my husband would bring me joy, however, this morning, he was the last person I wanted to speak to.

"How are you doing, Sweetheart?" he asked. It had been a long time since my husband had called me Sweetheart. I wondered why he was suddenly acting so nice.

"I'm fine," I whispered.

"Tina, I wanted to speak with you about getting our marriage back on track. I know you've been unhappy lately," he began.

I was so startled that I couldn't even talk to my husband. He gave me the phone number of his Italian hotel and I told him that I would return his call later.

"What's the matter, Tina?" Gerald whispered in my ear.

"That was Mark," I said.

"What does he want?" Gerald tightened his grip on my slim body as if he wanted to protect me from the wrath of my husband.

"He wants us to work out the problems in our marriage," I whispered. I was still shocked to hear that my husband wanted us to save our relationship. Whenever I told him about my unhappiness, he would always turn a deaf ear. However, now he wanted to get our marriage back on track. It just didn't make any sense.

"Remember what I said last night, Tina. I love you. Your husband doesn't deserve you. You're nice and you're beautiful. Your husband doesn't appreciate you."

I was glad to hear Gerald's declaration of love. However, I was confused too. I had loved my husband once. He had treated me like a princess and I fell in love with him. He used to be gentle and thoughtful, and back in the days when we were dating, he would make love to me constantly.

Now things were different. He'd acquired his international company shortly before we were married. Our marriage was not happy and I couldn't see things changing, that is, unless he found a job that allowed him to come home each night.

My husband was going to be in Italy for another couple of weeks and after that, he would be at home for a bit before he went on his next trip. Next month he was scheduled to be in China for three weeks. My husband's business was taking a toll on our marriage and I didn't know if there was any hope left for us.

I had my butler to prepare an elaborate breakfast for me and Gerald. I had him serve it on a silver tray in my bedroom. We feasted on crispy bacon and hot fluffy pancakes. Gerald had a healthy appetite. He again admonished me for not eating properly.

He stroked my thin arm as he looked at my plate of food, which I had barely touched. "Stop worrying about your husband. If you don't start eating regularly, you'll make yourself sick," he said wisely.

I made myself eat my pancakes and bacon. After we drank our strong black coffee, Gerald made love to me again.

I was glad when he left later that morning. I needed to be alone. I didn't return Mark's phone call. I still needed some time to think. I did call Gerald to let him know that I needed a few days alone though.

During the next few days I wondered if my marriage was worth saving. I walked around my huge mansion and touched the expensive items on the shelves.

If I divorced Mark, I would no longer be able to live in this mansion and I could no longer use his money. I would no longer have a butler and a maid at my disposal. Did I want to leave this life of luxury? I knew that Gerald loved me, and he owned his own pool-cleaning business, however, I knew he didn't make nearly as much money as Mark.

Would Gerald want to marry me if I did leave Mark? He said that he loved me, but he didn't mention anything about marriage.

I was surprised when I heard a knock at my door the next day. I opened the door and was surprised to see Kristine, Mark's personal secretary. She traveled with him to all of the foreign countries and they worked closely together while he was in the office here in the United States.

Kristine was a quiet, petite woman with long thick hair and large brown eyes. Her skin was the color of hazelnuts and her nails were as long as talons. She was wearing a pair of blue jeans and a big sweatshirt. This was the first time I had ever seen Kristine without her business suit.

"What's the matter? Did something happen to Mark?" My voice was full of alarm as she entered my home. Somehow I sensed that this was not a social visit.

She sighed. "Tina, we need to talk," she said.

"Okay," I replied. I had my butler bring coffee and cookies into the dining room. Kristine nibbled on a cookie, but she didn't touch the coffee. Her hands were shaking, as if she was nervous. "What did you need to talk to me about, Kristine?" I asked.

She sighed. "Tina, this isn't easy for me to tell you, but me and your husband have been having an affair for the past two years."

I gasped as I stood. "You're lying!" I spat.

"It's true," she said emphatically as she put her half-eaten cookie aside. She touched her abdomen as she continued to look at me. "I told him a few days ago that I was pregnant with his child, and he was able to get me fired from his company. Mark is a rich and powerful man. He said if I breathed a word about our affair to anyone, he would make sure that I never worked in this town again."

Tears came to my eyes as I listened to Kristine's words. Suddenly, everything made sense. Mark had called me from Italy, wanting to save our marriage a few days ago. He must have decided to patch

125

things up with me since his relationship with Kristine had ended. I was shaking with rage as I gazed at Kristine.

"How could you sleep with a married man?" I asked in a hoarse whisper.

I was surprised to see that Kristine was crying too. "Tina, I'm not proud of what I did. When Mark first hired me, he told me that he wasn't married and I believed him. Once I found out, we'd already started our affair and I'd already fallen in love with him. I'm sorry."

She then went on to say that she had a lot of contacts in the business world and that she was going to hire a lawyer to sue Mark's company for wrongful termination from her job. I gazed at Kristine. She wasn't much older than I. She looked sad and alone and now she had a baby on the way.

"Mark wanted me to get an abortion, but I refused. That's why he managed to get me fired," she said as she continued to sob. I could no longer be mad at Kristine. Mark had swindled her. He had used her for his sexual needs, and now he was unwilling to pay the price. Now I understood why he never wanted us to make love. Our marriage was over a long time ago, and I knew there was no way that we could repair the damage.

The next day Gerald came to the house to clean the pool. When he was finished, he came to the house for lunch. He looked as sexy as usual. We shared a long passionate kiss before he presented me with a bouquet of ruby red tulips.

"You make me feel so special," I whispered as I enjoyed the sweet fragrance of the flowers.

We weren't hungry for food that day. We skipped our meal as I led Gerald to the bedroom. I placed the flowers in vase and I opened the window. The bright sunlight spilled onto our heated bronzed bodies. He toyed with my nipples until they resembled tight chocolate peaks.

I ran my fingers over his strong back. I took the lead and got on top of him. As he continued to toy with my breasts with his large hands, I slid his organ inside of me and I moaned with pleasure. I loved having Gerald inside of me, loving me. My cries of ecstasy echoed throughout the room. I clung to his heated chocolate brown body when we were done.

"I love you so much, Tina," he whispered in my ear.

I rolled onto my back and gazed at his handsome face. His dark skin glistened and his lips were full and moist. He cupped my large breasts in his hands and licked my ear.

"You look tired. There are circles under your eyes," he observed.

I sighed and in a soft voice, I told him about Kristine's visit the previous day. He frowned as he looked at me. "I hope you're not planning on staying with that bastard," he spat.

"No, I don't want to stay with Mark any longer. But I can't end my marriage until I talk to him first. I have to find out what really happened between him and Kristine."

"You think she was lying?" asked Gerald.

He ran his fingers through my hair as he continued to cup by breast. Warm sensations traveled through my thin brown body. Gerald was a hot passionate man. He could arouse me with a kiss or a caress in an instant.

"No, but I just need to speak with Mark before I tell him about my decision," I said, my voice heavy with desire. He made love to me again at a slow, leisurely pace. When he was finished, he squeezed my body in his strong arms.

"Tina, leave Mark and marry me. I promise I will make you happy. I don't have all of this," he said waving his hands toward our lavish surroundings, "but I do make a good steady income from my pool-cleaning business. I promise I'll never cheat on you, and I'll come home and make love to you every night. Please say you'll be with me, Tina."

"Gerald, I'll let you know my answer as soon as I speak with Mark. I can't make a final decision until I do that."

"I don't think you should give that man another minute of your time, but I'll respect your wishes. After you speak with your husband, you can make a decision about spending your life with me."

"So you would definitely want to marry me?" I whispered.

He nodded. "Of course. You're a lovely woman Tina, and I love you. You would make me proud if you were my wife." I was so touched to hear his words. I made a promise to myself to call my husband the next day.

However, the following day, before I could make the phone call, Mark came walking through the front door. He had his luggage and his laptop computer. I was surprised because his trip was supposed to last another week. "Tina, sweetheart, it's so good to see you again. I want to make our marriage work. I've canceled my trip to China next month. I've decided to devote all of my spare time to you." He tried to hug me, but I pulled away.

"Mark, we really need to talk," I said.

"Baby, what's wrong?" He stared into my face. "You look like you've been crying." He tried to caress my cheek, but I turned away from him.

"Kristine came to visit me the other day," I announced. His brown eyes widened and his face slowly filled with rage.

"What did Kristine want?" he whispered.

"What do you think she wanted?"

"Don't believe anything she said, Tina! She's just mad because she got fired! She's an incompetent slut! We never had an affair!"

I gasped. My husband had just admitted his guilt. "I never said that she revealed anything about an affair," I whispered.

"Well...whatever she said, it's just not true!"

My husband couldn't say anything to cover his tracks now. He'd had an affair with Kristine and now she was pregnant with his child. While we were married, he had been sleeping with another woman while I lay alone in my bed most nights. While he was away in Paris, Rome, China, and Japan, my husband had been sleeping with his secretary.

"All I want to know is why, Mark. Why do you want me around anymore? We hardly ever make love anymore, I never see you. Why would you even want to save this marriage?" I whispered.

His silence was the only answer I needed. My husband wanted to patch things up with me because Kristine was no longer his mistress. "I'm seeing a lawyer tomorrow and I'm filing for a divorce," I announced.

"Over my dead body! I won't grant a divorce!"

"Yes you will! Besides, you were the one that was unfaithful." I did know that I would have any trouble getting a divorce.

"If you divorce me, you won't get any of my money," he said.

"I don't want your money," I spat. I quickly ran upstairs and packed a suitcase. I then called a cab and I went to Gerald's house. He welcomed me with open arms. He loved me all night and my gentle cries could be heard throughout his entire house.

After a year of separation, I did manage to divorce Mark. Kristine also found a lawyer to sue Mark's company. Both of us got good lawyers and I was able to get a handsome settlement from Mark since he was the one who had been unfaithful in our marriage.

Kristine was able to get a good settlement also, plus Mark had to pay child support until their baby was twenty-one years old.

As soon as my divorce was final, I married Gerald. We took a trip to Jamaica, his homeland. While standing on the white sandy beaches, we declared our love for one another and said our vows. I was ecstatic when we were pronounced man and wife.

We spent our honeymoon on this exquisite island and in the middle of the night, when the moon is shining and the stars are bright, Gerald made love to me on the white sandy beaches of his homeland. My cries carried over the wind as I proclaimed my love for my new husband.

THE END

SEX TRIANGLE
I Couldn't Get Enough Pleasure

I found the courage to quit my receptionist job with the renown law firm of Broodmoore, Donovan, Kerr & McGee. Two weeks later, I became an Andrew Martin Entertainment client. Although Mr. Martin respected my talent as a promising singer/song writer, he suggested we concentrate on polishing those talents after I completed three Public Service Announcements. Each was different, especially the first. That's how I met Charles Anthony Armstrong, a struggling New York actor.

According to the first script, Charles and I were fictional college students contemplating marriage and babies, but the central message of the psa was advocacy of prolonged condom use, if abstinence wasn't preferable. The scene was shot on location inside an LA Laundromat. It marked my debut as a paid actress, and Charles' fifth appearance in front of a film production camera. What I found so enjoyable was working with a talented female director who was a smooth operator when it came to directing. She was an excellent role model for me.

The project was concluded within eight hours. Afterward, Charles invited me out to eat dinner at McDonald's, which was a three block journey from the Laundromat. I was embarrassed while I watched him eat like a starved jungle beast. He was finished before I was half done with my Big Mac and fries. Now he was smiling at me, as if I were his prized audience.

"I bet you think I'm a slob, huh?"

"Not really."

"I've always been a fast eater. Almost like sex: instant gratification."

I rolled my eyes. "I'm glad you can't get indigestion that way."

His riotous laughter turned heads in our direction. Again, I was so embarrassed. I was hoping this wasn't a full time character trait he showed the world. Still, I didn't dislike him and considered him to be a very talented actor who, not unlike me, needed a big break.

We had discussed that situation soon after Mr. Martin first introduced us. Among other things, Charles claimed he was happily married with twin daughters, but during our break periods on the set he made numerous references about what a joy it would be to have me as a special friend; he emphasized "special" in such a way it was flat out sexual. I already was on guard in case he made it a point to continue throwing darts at the same target. Me!

I wasn't interested in him as a sex partner. I certainly wasn't going to arouse his curiosity by revealing that I hadn't enjoyed a satisfying intimate relationship with a man in fourteen months. Inspite of my intelligence, pleasant personality, good looks, stylish way of dressing, and having the ability to set and accomplish goals, I was dumped by a man who swore he loved me. At the time, I was only four months away from being a bride. What a fool I had become, all along not knowing he still was married but separated, all along loving him, pleasing him, planning with him what we envisioned to be a very bright and rewarding future.

He proved to be the ultimate liar soon after his estranged wife-having hired a private detective from Champaign, Illinois-revealed to me over the telephone about the pathetic history of their failed marriage. Fortunately, the misfortune wasn't weighty enough to sink my positive mental attitude toward meeting and falling in love with the proper man. I just had to be more cautious and patient and selective.

"Enjoying your ride on that cloud?"

"Excuse me?"

"You were riding on a cloud and not listening to me."

"I'm sorry. I was thinking about, uh, the future end results of our first, uh, project together. I hope it turns out to be both effective and successful."

He saluted me with a "thumbs up" gesture. "No problem. I hope the residuals keep coming for the next sixty years. By then, I'll be way beyond condom use."

I chuckled and he glanced at his watch. "I wonder if it's possible we can persuade Mr. Martin we should continue working as a team in the next two psa's." He began making galloping horse sounds with his fingers. It was a thinking habit gesture I first discovered off the set.

I shrugged. "Sorry, Charles. I'm powerless. Without control over the matter." I could tell he was staring at the menu board above the service counter. His gaze didn't waver even when a herd of rowdy preteens invaded us. I hoped he wasn't considering ordering more food, because I was eager to leave, return to my hotel room, sleep well, and tomorrow morning take a flight back to Albuquerque.

During the week of closing the psa deal through the agency, I had auditioned for an important role in a one-act play and was selected as a cast member. Now I was faced with a four week rehearsal schedule.

"I guess that means we won't be seeing each other again no time soon, huh?" His gaze into my eyes made me feel uncomfortable. I wanted to scratch my tingling scalp.

"I didn't say that, Charles."

"But you're not offering any encouragement, either."

I glanced at the other patrons. "I'll get straight to the point. I'm not seeking to start a relationship with you, other than work. Is that clear enough?"

Charles leaned back, sighed, and folded his arms against his chest.

"Look, Olinka, I didn't mean to crowd you into a corner. I just think you're special. I like you a lot." His sudden smile expressed several different meanings at once. "If you want just a basic friendship, well okay, that's cool with me." Yet something deeper in his eyes warned me that he wasn't going to quit trying to go beyond friendship.

I grabbed my shoulderbag. We rose together. I hadn't forgot we were registered at the same hotel but on different floors. I was truly thankful he made no attempts to pressure me into his wishful thinking during the remaining time we spent together.

The ball of success really started bouncing forward for me after the world premiere of the one-act play When Justice Throws The Second Stone.

It was a huge commercial and artistic success in Albuquerque. Local media reviews by critics were excellent. The drama was scheduled to end in September, but popular demand convinced the producer to hold it over for another two weeks. Afterward, it was scheduled to tour all over America for the next nine months. I wasn't sure I would be a touring cast member.

My life became a bigger rollercoaster ride because of the play's success . It seemed like every eligible bachelor in New Mexico wanted to wine and dine me. I received tons of greeting cards, enough flowers to open a floral shop, and offers from other entertainment agencies. I appeared on three local current affairs television programs. I was interviewed by a popular public radio hostess. I was invited to speak at charitable functions. One ambitious businessman wanted to hire me to pose bikini-clad to help him sell more used cars. I had little free time for myself anymore. I didn't resent what was happening to me, but I didn't want to encounter early burn-out, thereby harming my mental and physical health.

I didn't dwell on the fact too much that I didn't have a steady and reliable man in my life-a lover to come home to, one who would be loving, tender, affectionate, sensitive, and have the ability to make life seem less chaotic and challenging. The men I had met during the weeks of the premiere seemed clonish in one sense: they were more interested in me as a sex partner than anything else.

Time after time, their eyes reflected that same desire, all because I was big, tall, and good looking. What they didn't want to hang around long enough to discover was my capacity to love the proper man, deeply and unconditionally. I wasn't so callused to the point where I was going to give up my search for him. I assumed, justifiably so, that it would take years and years Unexpectedly, fate shined its sweet light on me much sooner.

Less than thirty minutes after I entered my apartment, the telephones started ringing. I was stretched out naked on the bedroom waterbed, half-asleep, and still tired from a final Sunday matinee performance of the play. I groped for the receiver, almost dropped it, and said, "Hello?" before I muffled a big yawn.

"Hello dear. Did I awaken you?"

"Oh. Hi Mr. Martin. Not at all."

"I promise I won't make your ear sore."

"I always enjoy talking with you."

"The play still remains a knockout success."

"Very much, sir," I muffled another yawn; it felt so good.

"Are you ready to tackle another project? Perhaps more ambitious."

I sat up. I felt tingly all over, more alert now. I sensed he was about to tell me something important. I wanted to giggle. I restrained my response. "I'm ready, as long as it doesn't involve terrorism."

We chuckled.

"Far removed from that kind of nasty business. Yesterday evening, I received a phone call from Keith Wey."

"Keith Wey, the tennis champ?"

"Former tennis champ. He retired three years ago."

"Oh. I guess I haven't kept up with his career."

Mr. Martin chuckled. "You're not alone."

The gears in my mind raced faster in attempt to figure out what the connection was between Keith Wey and Mr. Martin. The last facts I knew about Keith Wey was his decision to become a resident of France, where his French-born fiancee, a hot shot fashion photographer, was residing.

"Keith is now an independent filmmaker. To be precise: producer, director, writer."

"Hhmm. Well now. Interesting."

"He's at the production stage of a new feature film project. I'm not at liberty to divulge much more information than this. Based on reviews, he praised your talents in the Justice play. He's seeking an actress of your rising caliber to perform in a psychological thriller. Are you interested?"

"Of course! But, well, I wish you could give me more information. You know, Mr. Martin, this is so sudden. Like pennies falling from heaven."

"Indeed. Get yourself pen and paper. Then take it from there."

As I wrote down all pertinent information, my tears and mind

132

were in a wrestling match, making me naturally high.

"Be sure to contact Keith no later than Tuesday afternoon. His crew is scouting for-never mind. Sorry."

"Please, Mr. Martin. Don't stop. Tell me. I promise I won't reveal what you say." If my pulse rate was a buzzing smoke detector fire trucks would be racing to douse my blaze.

"Young lady, if you do I'll personally feed you to my pet alligator." Only I chuckled; he in contrast seemed deadly serious. "Vancouver, British Columbia is the principle locale."

"I haven't traveled there before."

"Not a word to anybody, Olinka, until after you speak with Keith. So rest well. Take your vitamins. Call me soon."

Because Mr. Martin was a wonderful conversationalist I was reluctant to hang up. I could talk with him for hours. Now a new challenge stood before me, waiting for me to grab its slippery horns.

I preferred to meet him in person, but my conversation with Keith Wey that fateful Monday morning was like a lifesaving shot in the arm. He wasn't unfriendly, mostly preoccupied, and just all about business in the way he articulated his production needs. I wasn't deceived by his smooth, soft spoken voice that left a smile on my face throughout the conversation. He promised I would have a copy of the script before Wednesday. He was as secretive with information as Mr. Martin had been.

The script arrived. I was intrigued not only by the title-Spiral-but also by the plot: Leeza Mackleroy, a bride to be, is mysteriously abandoned by her lover two weeks before they are to be married. In her mind there is no justification for his disappearance. She decides to conduct her own investigation, which leads her to Vancouver, British Columbia, where she receives the worst shock of her life.

The more I reread Spiral the more I convinced myself that I was talented enough to portray Leeza Mackleroy. Two days later, I contacted, Mr. Martin and he set up an appointment so we could further discuss business.

It was as if love at first sight was responsible for the strong emotional swell within me when I met Keith at his West Los Angeles production facility. Right then and there, shortly after he escorted me into his private office, and presented me a half dozen roses before I sat in front of his massive executive desk, my intuition warned me that we would be right for each other in building an intimate relationship. I couldn't help but stare at him, the once great tennis star with longish curly hair, a rugged but photogenic face that graced so many magazine covers. His proud nose and jutting chin seemed to compete in the name of impressionable arrogance, yet his mellow voice didn't belie that attitude.

"Is something wrong, Ms. Barbour?" His deep-set eyes studied me, as if he were a concerned surgeon and I his patient.

Never before had I felt so speechless, so bowled over by a man's over-all presence. "Oh no. Definitely not. I was just, you know, thinking about how wonderful it is to-do you always give a would-be auditioner roses?" My eyes were still determined to unflinch in admiration for him. Had he cast a spell on me? Was his personality that magnetic, irresistible? I sensed he was taking his time to respond appropriately.

"Believe it or not, you're the first. Mostly because I admire fresh, new talent. And the possibility of us working together as team players."

I nodded in agreement, so far enjoying every word he spoke. Now he was providing me with more information concerning the main character. Afterward, he and I read sections of the script. He asked for feedback and I provided enough to make him ask additional questions. After that, he set a date for my initial audition, which would be video taped by his crew.

What I least expected from Keith was an invitation to a home-cooked meal. I wondered had he extended the same invitation to other proposing, up-and-coming actresses. I asked him that and he said 'no.'

We exited his office. He introduced me to his crew and gave me a tour of the various departments that made up the production facility. Somehow, the whole affair made me more energized, more enthused, more eager to become better acquainted with Keith. Well, I got that opportunity after he drove me in his exotic sports car that traveled to his six-figure hillside party house.

Track lights from the ceiling in the spacious kitchen beamed down on me as I sat on a tall bar stool and caressed a glass of California white wine. I was watching him prepare our dinner, which would be shrimp fried rice Keith-style. One part of me still didn't want to believe that I was in the presence of a great tennis champion turned filmmaker seeking to produce and direct a hit movie. I wanted to ask him about his affair with the fashion photographer; I could only assume it was history and an experience to be forgotten. There was nothing in his office I was aware of that reminded him of his past lover. As for me, it had been a few years the last time I was seriously in love

"Getting hungrier?" Keith said in a teasing undertone. He was dicing more onions, green peppers, and brown mushrooms.

"I'm ready to eat just about anything." Including you, I thought, allowing my eyes to drink in the firm roundness of his butt in faded blue jeans. I was almost tempted to ease off the stool and ease up behind him. Then I would wrap my arms around his tapered waist, and squeeze him tenderly. He in turn would gaze deep into my loving eyes, and kiss me with all the passion stored in him because of not having the right moment to share it with the right woman-until my arrival.

"Dinner will be served in the next fifteen minutes, Olinka," he announced. "What's on your mind? You've been too quite lately."

"I'm thinking about my audition," I replied, feeling somewhat guilty for lying. "I'm a little nervous about the whole thing."

Keith turned and smiled at me. I thought my heart was going to melt at that very instance. "Don't worry. You'll do just fine. I believe in you." He winked. Then he began stir frying the concoction of diced ingredients. The business of cooking and the wonderful smells only made my stomach growl for satisfaction. It wasn't until he scrambled a half dozen eggs that I realized that this dinner was going to lead us to his bedroom. With such a guest like me, I honestly didn't believe he was going to sentence me to a guest bedroom adjacent to his.

Dinner was superb! A real treat for my taste buds! It made me appreciate Keith more than I anticipated. From the kitchen suite we settled in the swanky, super-spacious, sunken living room that reminded me of a playpen for adults. After about two hours of intense conversation, he excused himself. I just sat on the plush sectional sofa and listened to the blues music he loved dearly. I had less appreciation for it, but I was learning to like it because of him.

My eyes were closed in absorption of the complex composition. When I opened them, there stood Keith. He was smiling. Secured between his outstretched fingers was an alluring see-through nightgown. I was too surprised and a little off balance to offer an immediate response.

"No strings attached," he said. "I want you to look and feel comfortable. I assume you're spending the night with me. Unless you have objections."

I tried not to swallow the dry lump in my throat, but it happened anyway. "Well, since you're such a gentleman and a thoughtful one, I'm willing to stay overnight. But only on one condition."

"Such as?"

"I usually sleep in the nude when I'm alone. Which means I will wear your nightgown."

He smiled even bigger, breaking that momentary tension within himself.

"I can deal with that," he said. Because Keith was an early riser, we spent only two more hours discussing our past achievements, our hopes and dreams, and our outlook on the future. It was how he kissed me that inspired me to escort him into his sensational baronial-style bedroom crowned with wall and ceiling mirrors. It wasn't quite true but the low profile bed seemed to stretch from wall to wall. The tiger stripe spread was peeled back, exposing rich textured gold satin sheets.

"Very, very nice," I said, trying to maintain a cool and collective head. Already, though, my aching nipples were pressing against the cups of my bra, and my tongue was ready to sample the texture of his manly body still covered in clothing. "Now what?" My tone was just as nervous and unsure of what he expected from me?

"Don't remove your clothes. Allow me." He began unbuttoning his shirt. More flashing heat spread all over me when I saw his hairy, broad chest a little too eager, tapering down to his small waist. We were of equal height, and that fact pleased me, too. He came to where I stood. "You're a sculptor's dream come true." If his soft voice was brandy I'd be severely intoxicated by now. Within short seconds he had detached my blouse and removed it. He gazed proudly down my prominent cleavage and offered it a wet kiss. I heard myself suck in air when he removed my bra, then came my skirt and panties. Before he lifted me off the carpet and lowered me down onto the ocean of bed, he thanked me for trusting him and for not being uptight about expressing sexual desire.

At last, he removed his pants. My attention below his navel assured me that Keith was all man, had staying power, eager to please me beyond my wildest dreams. As he eased down beside me, he confessed, "I've been celibate for almost two years. How long for you?" He nibbled on my neck before he planted delicate kisses all over my hot face. I began massaging the back of his neck.

"One year. I still believe in safe sex. Regardless." As if my answer were a cue for him to make his next move, his lips and tongue traveled to my waiting breasts. He was too gentle and considerate as he enjoyed the taste of me-all the while moaning and smiling and growing hotter in the fingers. He ventured further below and spent much attentive time taking me on an around the world trip of fantastic pleasure.

Near the end, as the ceiling began to spin, I begged him to stop because I feared I'd have a heart attack. I needed some time to recover. Now it was my turn to show him how much I knew how to please a man like him. My erotic abandonment had him calling out my name. And after he secured himself with a condom an hour later, we made love the old-fashioned way: slow, easy, with much give and take.

Months later, I heard myself saying, "This is crazy, Mom! Absolutely crazy! He was suppose to call me yesterday. That was two weeks ago. Yeah-sure. I called everywhere. Police headquarters. Five hospitals. The Justice Center. Even a few funeral homes." I transferred the prop telephone to my other ear, ran fingers across my forehead as I stared through the picture window of the apartment Keith's production company had rented. It was as if I was expecting my screen lover to pull up to the curb in his sports car and offer me, the character I was portraying in the movie script, a logical explanation for his odd disappearance and disruption of our wedding day.

"Okay, Mom. I'll try to keep calm, but it's so hard not knowing the truth, not knowing where Alonzo is. What? Maybe. I'll try that, too, and see what happens. Sure. I'll let you know the outcome. I love you, Mom. Thanks for your support." I reluctantly lowered the receiver. When I began crying again, Keith yelled "Cut!! Great take! A fine, job, Olinka!"

Even the crew members praised my performance. We were at the halfway point in the script with this scene. Yesterday, Keith had announced that all of us would be heading to Vancouver, British Columbia the third week of April, when weather conditions would be ideal for a week's worth of filming the plot twists.

"Okay everybody," Keith said. "Let's eat lunch, then wrap up this sequence before three." At that moment a popular catering truck pulled into the apartment complex parking lot. While most of the crew headed to the truck, Keith and I settled in the kitchen and opened the brown bag lunches I had prepared at his house.

"If we keep making this kind of progress, we'll be about $60,000 under budget by the time we venture up north." He bit into his sandwich.

"Good news for your investors, right?"

"That, and my next project. Sorry, Olinka. Gotta keep it a secret for now."

As I was about to respond with a witty reply, the throaty sound of a powerful European sports car pulled into the parking lot and settled beside Keith's equally exotic sports car.

"Be cool, okay?" Keith warned me, as a strikingly pretty woman strided toward us. "She's only here to cause trouble."

"Who is she, Keith?"

"The French photographer."

"Oh, her." I watched how she smiled at Keith, who wasn't smiling. "I thought you and her were finished."

"That's a topic for later. Just be cool."

Keith's uninvited visitor wore designer sunglasses that reflected our images. Her body told the world that she was a health and exercise practitioner. I couldn't wait to hear the motive behind her sudden appearance.

"So you thought you could hide from me. You should know better, Keith."

"Olinka," Keith said, "I want you to meet Teena Riordan, a very gifted fashion photographer." Even after Keith revealed my name,

137

pouty Teena and I still didn't shake hands. We gave each other a respectful nod of recognition: no nonsense equals.

Teena lowered her sunglasses. Her bold, soulful eyes seemed to give my figure a closer inspection. I couldn't tell whether she approved or disapproved until she said, "You always did have good taste in women. Like plucking the finest grapes for superior winemaking." Her husky voice made me believe she was a serious cigarette smoker. I started to worry that her oversized bosom would escape from her halter top. Somehow, I sensed that she knew that I was Keith's new love interest. Her next remark took us by surprise.

"Has he bought you a diamond ring yet, Olinka?"

"Is that important for you to know, Ms. Riordan?"

Like two strange cats in a dark allay, we stared at each other for a moment.

"At least you got one that's snappy like a chili pepper," Teena said to Keith.

After Keith returned a crew member's signal that production would restart in five minutes, he asked Teena, "What brought you here?"

Suddenly, she was like a sweet little girl ready to sit on daddy's knee. "To spy on you before I return to Paris." Only she chuckled. "My flight leaves tomorrow morning. I had a two week shoot in LA-what a trip! I figured we could get reacquainted before I leave."

Yeah, right-in Keith's master bedroom, I thought in a flash of jealousy. I just couldn't imagine him making love to any other woman but me.

Now I was staring at this Teena Riordan-long-haired, pretty, intelligent, sexy who just then attempted to clasp Keith's hands into hers and guide him in a direction for intimate privacy. Unlike me especially deep inside-Keith was very cool-headed about the attempted gesture. Clearly, Teena resented the rebuke but she didn't verbally protest. I thanked the good Lord for that gesture of common sense.

Keith checked his watch. "Our break's almost over," Keith warned his ex lover. "I'm sorry, but we won't be spending any get-reacquainted-time together."

Teena pouted even more.

Keith glanced at me, with the look of genuine love stamped into his eyes. His smile melted my heart. "Besides, Olinka and I are getting married in June."

"Oh my God!" Teena sang.

Inwardly, I thought I had swallowed a gold fish, but outwardly I was as cool as a rainy winter day. There was not an ounce of truth to that statement. Yet it sounded so delicious, so promising, so thrilling. My brainstorming made me wonder did Keith have such thoughts about marriage and building a family. The more I thought about it, the more I felt inspired to give him much more of me.

"I suppose I can't keep this a secret from you much longer," Teena said to Keith. "I'm sure it won't break your heart. I got married last September."

Keith seemed stunned, lost for words.

"We're expecting our first child in June. Could have been yours, Keith. Luck of the draw, huh?"

"Congratulations," I said, so happy Teena would no longer by my competitor for Keith's love and affection.

"Congratulations to you and Keith," Teena said. "I hope you live long lives together." She kissed Keith on the cheek, tenderly squeezed his hand, and then calmly drove out of our lives forever.

It was funny how we almost sighed in relief at the same time. The announcement of a fictional June wedding made us laugh all the way to the set.

Finally, the third week of April arrived. I was as eager to depart LA as wild horses breaking free from a burning corral. Now, only eight hours separated us from the start of our important destination. The technical production crew had already settled up there, which meant only five of us had to board a jumbo jet. A much tougher schedule lie ahead, Keith had often warned me, but I still was game and ready for the challenges. It dawned on me that his statement had another meaning: the possibility of less intimacy between us during the three weeks of filming on location. Therefore, I initiated something I hadn't tried before.

When I opened my eyes the digital nightstand clock showed 2:17 A.M. I snuggled against his back. I nibbled on his ear. He moaned words that seemed to express his annoyance. When it came clear to him what was really happening, he shook his head, said forget it, and abruptly removed my fingers from his manhood.

Of course I wasn't going to quit. Besides, I was having fun and the urge deep within me needed to be satisfied. So I reached down and grasped him after I repositioned my body. The warmth of my lips and mouth greeted him. No response came the first few minutes, but the transformation was right on time after I worked on him with much more enthusiasm.

Now Keith was urging me not to stop pleasuring and I didn't until he pulled me on top of him. He joined me in one quick motion which took my breath away and made me squeeze my eyes shut. We hugged each other as we moved like a well-oiled machine built for speed and endurance. I cried out his name each and every time he thrusted deeper inside me. That wonderful ball of fire was growing larger and hotter.

We started kissing as if it were our last day on earth. The pleasure was so intense for so long, but I forced my lips from his and began bouncing against his thrusting. A thousand crazy fingers seemed to be stroking me all over. And when he massaged my aching nipples I thought I was going to faint!

Then the inevitable happened: pure, raw, spin-tingling climaxes that led to sleep so sweet, so heavenly. I had found the man of my dreams after all.

THE END

I LOVED BEING
THE OTHER WOMAN

I couldn't stand Gina Langley. She thought she ruled the campus, with her good looks and fancy clothes. She might've been the most popular girl on campus, but one thing was certain: she wasn't going to keep that good-looking boyfriend of hers—Carlos Harrell. I was determined to make him mine.

Carlos Harrell had a few business classes with me. I was surprised when I learned that his girlfriend was Gina. They were so different that I couldn't understand how they had gotten together. Gina was arrogant and self-centered and Carlos was always friendly and warm whenever you saw him.

Once I learned that Carlos worked part-time at a service station near campus, I began to frequent it.

"Could you check the oil for me please?" I asked Carlos before I paid him for my gas.

"Sure thing, Shana," he said with a smile.

"Why is it I don't ever see you out at the usual hangouts?"

"I'm either working or studying, I guess. Then I spend a lot of time with my girl, Gina."

"She's one lucky lady to have someone like you to keep her company."

Carlos said nothing. He gave me a wry grin.

"You two have been going together about a year now, I understand. Isn't it about time for you to give someone else a chance?"

"And would that someone be you?" He rested against my car, wiping his hands.

"Would that be so bad? I think you're kind of fine."

"You sure are different from the girls on campus. I'm used to playing games when it comes to a girl saying what's on her mind."

"I haven't considered myself a girl since I left high school." I stood in a manner to show off my shapely figure.

Carlos assessed me hungrily with his eyes. I could tell by his appreciative look that he didn't see me as a girl, either.

"So, how about giving up your little girlfriend for one night with me? I can guarantee it will be an evening you won't forget."

Carlos became speechless. It was obvious he wasn't used to a woman being straight with him.

"Think about it some. Here's my phone number and address.

Give me a call when you're ready for a real woman."

When I gave him the slip of paper, he took it reluctantly.

I got in my car and I winked at him before I sped off the gas station lot. In my rearview mirror, I could see Carlos standing in the same spot, watching me with a silly grin.

By the time I got to the campus grill to meet my friend, Jewel, I was bursting with excitement.

"What's going on, Shana?" Jewel asked.

"I did it! I did it!" I exclaimed.

"You did what?" Jewel asked, sitting up straight in her seat.

"I went up to Carlos Harrell and told him I was interested in him."

Jewel leaned toward me. There was nothing she liked better than a hot piece of news.

"Did he fall for it?" asked Jewel. She knew about my plan to get even with Gina.

"I've got him going. I think it will take a few days for him to give me a call, but he will."

"I can't wait to see how this will work out." Jewel's eyes widened with excitement.

"It'll work out just fine. Gina will be outdone when she realizes that I'm the fat Teresa she used to tease in school. The one she embarrassed so badly that I would go home and cry. I hated myself and I dreaded going to school because of her."

"You've been carrying this grudge ever since high school?"

"That's right. I've never forgotten how mean she was to me. Who'd ever thought we'd wind up at the same college?"

"Before you transferred schools, you were known as Teresa Bell—never Shana."

I nodded. "Teresa is my first name, I'm named after my grandmother. When I changed schools, I lost weight and changed my name to get rid of the bad things that I associated with being Teresa."

"When I see how hot you are now, I still can't believe that you were fat or ugly," said Jewel.

"Since I've lost weight, a lot of people don't recognize me. I'm sixty pounds lighter with a different color hair."

"Carlos and Gina are pretty tight. Do you really want to come between them?" asked Jewel thoughtfully.

"I sure do. Gina has to know what it feels like to be humiliated. I can't wait to see the look on her uppity little face when she loses her man to me."

"I only have one problem with this. If you're only getting even with Gina, where does this leave Carlos?"

"I don't really care. He's a big boy and he should be able to take care of himself. Besides, he deserves better than Gina."

"The whole thing sounds cold-hearted," she said.

"You call it cold-hearted, I call it revenge."

It took Carlos a couple of weeks to call me, but he did. Ever since that afternoon I gave him my number, I made it my business to be somewhere where he could see me. In order to entice him, I always dressed my sexiest. I gave him hot looks to make him think about me.

When Carlos began returning my smoldering looks, I knew it would only be a matter of time before my plan would go in effect.

One time when I caught him watching me, I mouthed the words "call me" and I blew him a kiss. Even though he was with Gina, he gave me a look that let me know I was wearing him down.

One afternoon, when I was cleaning up my apartment, Carlos called to ask if he could come over. It was just the call I had been waiting for.

I felt victorious as I went through my clothes, trying to find something sexy to wear. I decided to wear my sexy aerobic tights that were cut thigh high.

Carlos smiled awkwardly when I greeted him at the door. I invited him in and pretended to be cooling down from my exercise.

While he made himself comfortable on the sofa, I bent and stretched suggestively in my provocative outfit.

"So things are not going so good between you and Gina," I said as I sat Indian style in front of him on the floor.

Carlos chuckled. "I came here to see you, not to talk about Gina." He looked at me as if he were really seeing me for the first time

"I see," I said. "C'mon in the kitchen and I'll fix us a cold drink."

Carlos bounded from his seat and followed me into the kitchen. He stood close beside as I stood with the refrigerator door open, trying to decide what to serve.

"I'll take one of these," Carlos said, reaching in front of me for a can of beer. When he did, his arm brushed against my breast and he jumped back like he had been burned.

"It's okay, Carlos. Relax, I won't have you arrested."

He popped the top on the can and looked at me intently as he leaned against the counter. "What do you want with me, Shana? I mean, a fine lady like you who can have any guy on campus, yet you keep sending me these vibes to check you out."

My heart began to pound. For the first time since I met Carlos, I began to see him as more than just Gina's boyfriend. He was fine and he had a nice body, too. His eyes were the color of caramel and they were gorgeous.

Standing in front of Carlos, I took the can of beer out of his hand and pressed my body to his. His arms went around my waist without any qualms.

"I think we could be good together. Like I told you before, I don't think Gina gives you what you need," I whispered in a sultry voice

"And what is it that I need, lady?"

I placed my arms around his neck and I licked his sensuous lips. He looked as if I had hypnotized him. When my tongue entered his mouth, he was mine. His arms held me snugly to him.

"Carlos, you act like a man who is hungry for some real loving," I said, catching my breath from the hot, sweet kiss.

My knees were trembling and I had to step away from him to gain my composure. It wasn't supposed to be this way. I wasn't supposed to become involved with him, I thought. I led the way back into the living room and sat on the sofa.

Carlos sat close beside me. He began to rub his hands through my hair. I leaned my head on his chest and heard his heart beating like a bass drum. I caressed the side of his face and then we began to kiss until we could feel the heat coming from our bodies. When Carlos began to ease the top of my aerobic tights down, I didn't resist him. He was doing exactly what I wanted him to.

Carlos hurried out of his clothes without taking his hungry eyes off me. In a matter of seconds, he was beside me and then above me, hot and ready for loving

I stroked his muscled arms and ran my hands up and down his back Carlos cupped my breasts and kissed them until my nipples were hardened. I was floating on a cloud of ecstasy. I never dreamed that Carlos would be such a dynamite lover. Once our bodies became one, I knew that Carlos was the love I had been waiting for all my life. Consumed with passion, I realized I wanted Carlos for myself. I was no longer playing the game of getting even.

Carlos breathed hotly in my ear as we rose and fell with our fiery passion. When he looked into my eyes, I could see that I was taking him to a place where he hadn't been. He thrilled me through and through with his lips—with his hands. And when we'd stretched our passion to its limit, he held me tighter still as he called out my name.

As the sun began to peek through my window, I stood looking down at Carlos. I wondered if he could come to love me more than he did Gina.

Carlos must have felt me staring. He began rubbing the sleep from his eyes. He looked at me and smiled. I sat on the bed beside him; I lavished his chest with kisses

"That was some night," I said in a sultry voice.

"Damn good," he agreed. His voice was husky with sleep. He sat up and looked at the clock and saw that it was almost eight.

"I got to get out of here. I have an exam at one o'clock."

Carlos moved quickly from the bed

I watched him as he dressed; I hated to see him cover that fantastic body of his.

"Will you be back tonight? It could be just as good tonight."

He gave me an apologetic look. "I'm supposed to see—Gina tonight."

"Oh, I see." I tried to hide my disappointment.

When Carlos stood in the mirror to comb his hair, I slipped up behind him and slipped my hands in his front pockets.

"Give me a break, Shana." He laughed.

He removed my hands and whirled around and kissed me.

"Give Gina up. It's obvious that she's not that important to you anymore. If she was, you wouldn't have been able to give yourself to me the way you did. In fact, you wouldn't have even come here."

"You do have a point, but it's not as easy as that," said Carlos.

"I want us to be more than a hot night of passion."

"It won't be a one-night stand. I'll make time for you until I can make my break with Gina," he promised.

"Just make sure you do it soon. I don't want to have to share you any longer than I have to."

He kissed me before he left without making any definite plans.

As I watched him walk out the door, my stomach tied in knots. The fear of losing him to Gina consumed me

Although I was against keeping my relationship a secret, I didn't want to do anything that would jeopardize the way I felt about him. I had no other choice but to remain patient.

Carlos made it to my place when he could. It was usually late at night or midday when both of us had a break from classes. Whenever we were together, we made wild, passionate love. Neither one of us could get enough of the other.

One morning, while I was in the campus rest room, fixing my makeup, Gina walked in. She set her things on the sink next to mine.

"You don't remember me, do you?" I asked. I couldn't resist the chance to let her know who I was.

Gina stood with her cosmetic bag poised in her hand and stared at me.

"I'm Teresa Bell—the fat girl you used to tease in high school."

Gina's mouth fell open. "Why, it sure is you. Well, I'll be. Oh, girl, you really look good since you lost all that weight. I know you almost lost the size of another person, didn't you, girl?" She chuckled and made a sudden turn to put on her makeup. When she did, she knocked her purse to the floor and all of her things scattered on the floor.

Reluctantly, I knelt to help her. When I picked up her wallet, it fell open to a picture of Carlos.

"Who is this good-looking guy?" I asked, pretending to be dumb.

"That's my sweetie, Carlos." She smiled briefly and then the smile faded.

"He's fine. It must be hard to keep a good-looking man like that."

Sadness filled her eyes, but she tried to play it off.

"No, I don't have that problem. The only trouble is being able to spend enough time with him. He works part—time and he spends a lot of time studying—too much time." She gave me a frozen smile

"Sounds like trouble to me. I had a boyfriend who tried to hand me that

same kind of stuff. Came to find out he was spending his time with another woman," I lied to fill her with more doubt.

"Well, Carlos loves me. He'd never cheat on me. He'd never do a thing like that," said Gina. She sounded like she was trying to convince herself.

I loved seeing the insecurity that filled her face. For a second, I was tempted to tell her I was sleeping with her man. I could tell she really loved Carlos. The pain of losing him would deflate that big ego, I mused. And that's exactly what I wanted.

That evening, I went to Carlos' place uninvited. I knew his roommate was out and it was ideal for what I had in mind. Up until this time, I had never been to his place. I knew Carlos feared Gina coming by and finding me there. I didn't care if she did find me there. It would make things that much easier for me.

"Shana, what are you doing here? I'm getting ready to go out." He stood in the door with only his jeans on.

"No, you're not, either," I said, pushing my way into his place. I cornered him up against the door and began licking hair on his chest.

"You're not playing fair." His arms went around my waist

"All is fair in love and war, baby," I said. I kissed him with a deep passion.

"I was about to take a bath," he whispered.

"Sounds like a good idea."

The sides of his mouth tilted up at my words. He took my hand and led the way.

I began to unfasten my clothes as I followed him into the bathroom.

Carlos filled his large tub with warm, bubbly water. He got in first and then I sat in front of him. He lathered his hands with the sweet-smelling suds. He glided his magnificent hands from my back to the insides of my thighs. A delicious sensation shot through my body. I rested my head on his chest to make it easy for us to kiss. He cupped my wet, silky, smooth breasts until my nipples peaked. Nothing had ever felt so delicious. Water sloshed over the sides of the tub as I moved on top of him. As our bodies became one, a fire spread through me. We caressed and thrilled each other like fine-tuned instruments. Each moment in his arms had its own vital strength. My body burned and so did his as a golden wave of passion made our bodies tremble in ecstasy.

That night, Carlos forgot all about Gina. That night he wouldn't let me leave his side.

Two weeks later, while I waited for Carlos to come over, he called to tell me he couldn't make it. He didn't have to explain why because I knew it was probably Gina. I assumed that he had to make up to her all the broken dates he'd made with her to be with me instead.

I was furious when I hung up the phone. It was the second date he'd broken that week. It made me feel as though he was trying to get away from me instead of breaking up with Gina like he promised. Determined not to sit alone in my apartment, I dressed and headed to the mall to do some shopping I had put off.

The mall was crowded with shoppers, but it wasn't too crowded for me to see Gina and Carlos. They were standing in front of the jewelry store window, looking at engagement rings!

I rushed over to where they stood, holding hands. I shoved Carlos on the shoulder angrily.

"So this is the reason why you couldn't keep our date," I said. I eyed Gina.

Carlos was startled to see me.

"What are you talking about, Teresa?" asked Gina, using the name that she'd taunted me by.

"Do you want to tell her, Carlos, or should I?"

Carlos wouldn't look at me.

"Carlos and I have been seeing each other—we're lovers," I said.

Gina closed her eyes and she looked as if I had slapped her.

"Is this true, Carlos? Have you been with her?"

"We need to talk, Gina. This isn't the time or the place for that. Let's go to my place," said Carlos. He grabbed Gina by the arm; he gave me a helpless look as he tried to lead the now baffled Gina out of the mall.

Gina pulled away from him and came to me. "You'll never get Carlos. You're not his type, Teresa. Just because you lost weight doesn't change who you are and where you came from." Her eyes flashed with anger and fear.

Carlos stood looking at Gina as if he hadn't seen her before. I was glad the he had a chance to see how vicious she could be.

As I watched them walk away, I found myself wondering if Carlos would tell he the truth about us. I wondered if I were going to be the one to get hurt in the web of pain I had constructed for Gina.

Later that evening, I tried to call Carlos at his place, but there was no answer. I called him until I fell asleep crying.

The next day, I waited for him to call. When I didn't hear anything, I dressed and went to his house.

I was in for a big surprise when Carlos' roommate came to the door. He told me he hadn't seen Carlos. His bed was unslept in, he said. He told me to check back later, because on the weekends, he usually crashed with his girlfriend.

The words sent shivers up my spine. Carlos had spent the night at Gina's. That meant that again she'd gotten the best of me. But this time we weren't playing children's dirty games. This time the stakes were high. We were dealing in hopes and dreams—my future happiness.

When I returned to my car, Carlos pulled up in his car. He looked horrible.

"I was just looking for you. Your roomie told me you were probably at your girlfriend's."

"Shana, don't start with me. I've got a lot on my mind," said Carlos as he leaned on my car.

"Well, did you tell her? Did you tell Gina about us?"

"I think you took care of that." He sighed heavily. "What is going on between you two? I had no idea you two knew each other so well."

"We were in high school together, that's all."

"What kind of head games are you playing with me, anyway? Gina kept calling you Teresa."

"That's my real name. Shana is the name I like best. The one I chose to use when I started college."

"There's a rivalry between you two. Something is going on and neither one of you is being honest with me."

"There isn't any rivalry," I said. "She'd hate to lose anything to me. She feels that she's better than me. She did when we were in high school and she does now."

"Why is that, Shana?" Carlos stood up and looked at me

"Gina is used to having her way. She can't accept the fact that, at last, I can beat her at her own game—humiliation."

"Is that all I am to both of you? A pawn in a cat fight?" His voice was filled with anger.

"No, baby. I mean, in the beginning, I was only out to hurt Gina. She humiliated me so badly in high school. But the more I got to know you, the more I realized I needed you. I love you, Carlos. I can make your life so much more happier than she can." My arms were around his waist.

"I told her about us, Shana. She went to pieces. She locked herself in the bathroom and she tried to—" He paused as if try and calm himself. "She tried to slash her wrists."

A feeling of shame and defeat rushed through me. "I'm sorry to hear that. Is she all right?" I'd never expected her to physically hurt herself.

"I was able to bandage her wrists and get her to the emergency room. They decided to keep her for a couple of days because of what she tried."

Silently, we stood holding each other. Tears began to well in my eye. Carlos was lost to me now. I could feel it.

"Shana, I can't leave Gina now. I couldn't live with myself if she tried to harm herself again."

"But what about us? You love me—you can't deny that."

"I do, but Shana, you're strong. You can cope, baby. Let's just call a time out for a while and in a few months, maybe Gina will be more rational and then I can make my break."

I stepped away from him. "Carlos, you can't drop me like this. You make a choice now or forget about me."

"Don't be so heartless. Gina needs me to stand beside her."

I headed for my car and got in. Carlos was beside me.

"Shana, baby, please bear with me. We'll be together in time."

I looked at Carlos intently. Tears were meeting under my chin. "You don't love me. I don't think you ever did. It was just a physical thing for you." I swallowed hard and rested my head on the steering wheel for a moment to ease my aching heart. "I can't promise you that I'll wait. I have a feeling there will always be an excuse for you not to leave her, and I refuse to walk in Gina's shadow. It's too lonely, too painful, Carlos."

He didn't say anything. He reached out to take my hand and I shrugged it off.

"I loved you, Shana. I want you to know this."

As I pulled off the lot, my heart grew heavy with pain. I had given so much of myself for so little in return. But I have learned that another person's happiness can't be based on someone else's unhappiness. In the end, you're the one left with the pain and the shame.

THE END

Made in the USA
Middletown, DE
29 July 2015